P9-DTQ-958

Liam's hiding a terrible secret

"Go on, Dad," Molly prompted. "Liam and Brian were on the top of a cliff with the horses . . . then what?"

"Well, a storm came up suddenly. Brian's horse became terrified at the thunder and lightning. She reared again and again, and then lost her footing. Brian's horse crashed over the side of the cliff and landed on the beach."

Molly gasped. "And Brian?"

Mr. Morgan nodded darkly. "He and the horse were found on the beach, dead."

"Oh, no," Molly cried. "How sad. What about Liam?"

"Liam was found lying unconscious against a rock. He remained in a coma for two days. They didn't know if he would make it at all."

"But he did," Molly interjected. "He's not all right, though, is he?"

"He seemed to improve pretty rapidly until they told him about Brian's death."

"And then?" Molly prodded.

Her father smiled sadly. "He retreated into a shell. Now he can't—won't—speak."

ADAM SCHOOL
RIF

The Snow Angel

FOREVER ANGELS

The Snow Angel

Suzanne Weyn

This edition published in 2001.

Text copyright © 1997 by Chardiet Unlimited, Inc., and Suzanne Weyn.
Cover illustration copyright © 1997 by Mark English.
Cover border photography by Katrina.

Published by Troll Communications L.L.C.

All rights reserved. No part of this book may be reproduced or utilized
in any form or by any means, electronic or mechanical, including
photocopying, recording, or by any information storage and retrieval
system, without written permission from the publisher.

Printed in Canada.

10 9 8 7 6 5 4 3 2

*For Yolanda Gonzalez, an angel of
hospitality, care, and thoughtfulness,
with thanks for all you do.*
        —SW

1

"Who's that with Dad?" Molly Morgan asked as she pushed aside the velvet, cranberry-colored living room drapes and peered out the front window. She'd risen unusually early for a Saturday morning in excited anticipation of her father's return, and she felt as if she'd been waiting for days. When the gleaming limo finally pulled up to the house, Molly had expected her father to be alone. With her delicate nose nearly touching the glass, she watched her broad-shouldered father bend forward to assist the other person out of the limo. Molly leaned to the right to get a better look at the unexpected stranger.

A thin, dark-haired boy emerged. Molly guessed he was about her own age, thirteen. He had to be cold in the worn-looking green woolen jacket he wore. Molly even thought she saw a shiver shake his reedy frame.

Joy, the Morgan family's housekeeper, came alongside Molly and gazed out. "I've never seen *him* before," she observed thoughtfully. Joy, a rather stout woman, was no taller than Molly. She turned and looked into Molly's sea-green eyes. "It's a mystery to me. Why don't you go outside and find out."

Filled with curiosity and eager to see her father again after his three weeks away, Molly dashed to the front hall closet and pulled out her teal-blue parka. She flipped her long, white-blonde hair out from under the jacket's fake fur collar as she pulled open the heavy front door.

As soon as she was down the wide front steps, she turned off the flagstone walkway into the snowy front yard to cut a faster, diagonal path to her father. She hadn't bothered about boots, and the snow stung as it found its way into the tops of her socks and sneakers.

With slow, halting steps, Mr. Morgan helped the boy up toward the walkway while a burly, uniformed chauffeur took suitcases from the trunk. He was a big man with carrot-colored hair. Molly had never seen him before. She wondered for a moment why Franklin, their regular driver, wasn't driving. But all thoughts vanished from her mind when her father looked up and smiled warmly at her.

"My girl!" he called to her, the last word revealing his British accent.

Clouds of snow flew behind Molly as she ran to him. Oh, how she'd missed him while he'd been in Ireland painting. Ever since he'd given up his position on the stock exchange to fulfill his lifelong dream of becoming a painter, they'd become much closer. It was as if he'd become a new person, warmer and happier than he'd ever been before—the kind of father she'd always longed for. Looking at him now with his dark but graying hair longer than she'd ever seen it and his demeanor so much more relaxed, she felt a strong surge of happiness and love for him.

Molly wrapped her arms around her father's waist. "It's so good to have you home."

"It feels good to be home," he assured her. Then Mr. Morgan turned toward his companion. "This is Liam McDermott."

"Hi, Liam." With her arms still wrapped around her father, Molly scrutinized the boy, smiling in an effort to soften the effect of her inquiring stare. There was something odd about him. What was it? She couldn't tell.

He was certainly good-looking enough. A little gangly, perhaps, with long arms that hung a bit lifelessly at his sides. His pale, ungloved hands were sensitive-looking, as if he could some day be a sculptor or a pianist.

A light wash of freckles covered his face. Thick, curly, nearly black hair tumbled carelessly over deep blue, heavily lashed eyes. Yet, his oddly blank gaze didn't seem to take her in. His expression remained strangely immobile. Did he even realize she was there?

Was he blind?

But even if he were, couldn't he hear her? She'd said hi, yet he hadn't responded.

With a questioning expression, Molly looked to her father. The frowning glance he returned to her was troubled and seemed to warn her off further questions.

She was dying to know who this mysterious boy was. What was wrong with Liam? And why was he here?

"Liam will be staying with us for a few weeks," Mr.

Morgan explained, his reply frustratingly incomplete.

Molly cocked her head to the side and squinted at her father. Why? her eyes asked while her mouth replied, "That will be lovely."

With painstaking care, Mr. Morgan continued moving Liam toward the door as if, in fact, the boy were blind. He held one frail elbow in his steady hand and carefully guided Liam along the icy path. For his part, the boy allowed himself to be led, like a sleepwalker. "Liam is the son of my childhood friend Conor McDermott," Mr. Morgan continued.

"You mean a friend back from the time when you lived in Ireland?" Molly asked, hopping and weaving impatiently behind them. It was hard to walk at the same crawl as her father and Liam when she was so eager and excited to hear everything.

Mr. Morgan nodded. "Yes, we were in school together before I was packed off to boarding school in London."

Molly knew that sad story. After his Irish mother had died—Molly's grandmother, whom she'd never met but very much resembled—Mr. Morgan's stern English father sent him to boarding school, where he'd been miserable, lonely, and discouraged from becoming a painter.

They reached the impressively high front entranceway of the Morgans' imposing white brick home. "Is your mother home?" Mr. Morgan asked as he ushered Liam through the door.

"No, she's at her Daughters of Heritage meeting," Molly told him.

He smiled and rolled his blue eyes. She chuckled

along. Daughters of Heritage was a group of women whose family lineage in the United States could be traced all the way back to before the Revolutionary War. Somehow these women seemed to think that this fact made them special. Molly thought it was all pretty silly.

"I think someone's making a speech about how you can research your family tree or learn about your relatives or something like that," she added.

"Whatever makes her happy," Mr. Morgan said indulgently.

Joy hurried into the living room to greet them. "Welcome home, Mr. Morgan!" She hovered, waiting for his overcoat.

"Hello, Joy. Meet Liam McDermott, our houseguest," Mr. Morgan said, shrugging off his coat and handing it to the housekeeper.

"Hello." Joy greeted the boy, her friendly voice trailing off as she took in his blank demeanor. She, too, shot Mr. Morgan an inquiring glance as it became clear that Liam was not about to answer her.

Mr. Morgan put his arms protectively around Liam's slim shoulders. "Liam's had some hard times lately. I'm hoping we can help him while he's here."

This bit of information was so intriguing that Molly felt she might burst if she didn't get the whole story. She didn't want to offend Liam by asking rude questions, though. She couldn't tell if he could see or hear her, but her father was talking in a guarded way, as if he could.

The red-haired chauffeur came in laden with suitcases and set them down in the hall. He smiled and tipped his hat before leaving. Molly noticed that he had small, but twinkling, deep blue eyes. *And he has a kind face*, she thought as she watched the door close behind him.

"I brought back a few things for you," Mr. Morgan told Molly, nodding toward the matching monogrammed luggage.

"Thanks," she said, glancing at the suitcases. Normally she'd have been eager to receive her gifts, but now they didn't seem half as interesting as finding out about Liam.

"How about some lunch?" Joy offered. "I made a shrimp bisque to help take the chill out of your bones."

"No, thanks." Molly declined quickly. She was too excited and fascinated by this strange boy to think of eating.

"Have something, Molly," Mr. Morgan urged with gentle firmness.

Molly felt a quick snap of irritation. She knew that her father was still concerned about her anorexia. Not long ago, the disease had made her think she was gaining too much weight, even as her frail frame wasted away. But she'd come so far since then. Although still thin, she was no longer dangerously skinny, nor was she in danger of starving herself to death. Couldn't her father see that she had the eating disorder under control?

She opened her mouth to protest, then decided against it. She didn't want to argue with her father now.

"The soup is really delicious," Joy coaxed.

"I'll join you for a bowl as soon as I get Liam settled in the guest room," Mr. Morgan added, starting the boy up the gleaming wooden stairs. "The flight was long and he must be tired."

"All right," Molly agreed.

"Would the young man like some soup brought to his room?" Joy inquired politely.

"That sounds nice," Mr. Morgan answered for him.

Molly and Joy headed toward the kitchen together. "Well?" Joy asked after they had closed the pocket door that separated the kitchen from the living room. "Who is he?"

Molly filled her in on the little she knew.

"I'd guess he can see," Joy considered. "I saw his eyes move several times. I couldn't tell if he could hear or not, though. Maybe the poor boy's in shock."

"Shock?" Molly asked.

"Yes, you know," Joy said, lighting the stove burner under a shining kettle of soup. "When something terrible happens to a person, sometimes they can't get over it. They're in a state of shock."

"No," Molly said, interested by this new idea, but finding it a little too dramatic to be true. "Do you think so?"

"It could be," Joy insisted. "People in shock act like they're in a sort of daze. That boy certainly looked dazed."

"I wonder what could have happened to him," Molly pondered aloud.

When the soup was bubbling, Joy took a bowl of it to the sunny breakfast nook adjacent to the kitchen. She set the bowl on a table nestled in a green leather booth. Molly slipped into the booth, waiting for her father to join her, as Joy placed a steaming bowl of soup on a tray and carried it up to Liam's room.

Thoughtfully, Molly gazed out the window at the

snowy backyard scene. The square-cut hedges were blanketed in snow. The fountain in the center of the yard, long since drained for the winter, glistened with a glaze of shining ice.

What had happened to Liam? Why was he here? Molly burned to know. Why was her father taking so long to come down? She had a million questions for him, and she was determined not to let him out of her sight until he had answered every one.

2

Katie Nelson rummaged through the utensil drawer until she found a plastic fork. She went over to the stove and picked at the still-warm canned corned beef hash sitting in the frying pan. She'd come in starving from an early-morning editorial meeting for the school yearbook and found the house empty. Her twenty-year-old cousin, Mel, had probably left the hash on the stove. Mel loved to eat corned beef hash for breakfast, and he never cleaned up after himself.

The phone on the kitchen wall rang, and Katie snapped it up. "Hello?" she inquired, her mouth still full of corned beef hash.

"It's me, Christina," her friend Christina Kramer answered on the other end of the line. "How'd the meeting go?"

Katie walked back to the stove, stretching the cord on the phone as far as possible to make it reach. With the receiver cradled between her chin and shoulder, she filled her friend in on all that had happened while she continued to eat. "The kids really want that stupid 'Most Popular' column, so it looks like we're going to do it," she told Christina. Christina was on the yearbook staff, too, but hadn't attended the meeting because she had a cold.

"Why would they want to put in something so . . . weird?" Christina asked.

"Because they're morons," Katie answered, absently twisting her long auburn hair into a tight coil. "I'm in charge of a bunch of idiots, that's why!"

"You don't really think that, do you?" Christina asked.

"No, I guess not," Katie conceded more rationally. "I'm just annoyed with them right now. I really don't know what to think."

"It's so dumb," Christina sighed. "Why should we categorize people like that? Why do we have to attach labels to everything? Can't we just let people be? It's so . . . not karmic."

"So *what?*" Katie spluttered, letting her coiled hair spin loose and fall into soft auburn waves around her shoulders.

"Karmic," Christina repeated. "You know. What goes around comes around. As you sow, so shall you reap. What you do comes back to you."

Katie frowned down at the greasy food in the pan. "You are what you eat?"

"Yes, like that," Christina agreed.

"Yuck," Katie murmured, dropping her fork into the pan on the stove.

"Labeling people at our age is like not letting the universe unfold naturally," Christina continued. "It stops us from becoming who we'll be before we even get the chance to start becoming it. We should just be ourselves now, because when we get older people will be labeling us all the time."

Katie moved to a kitchen chair closer to the phone as she listened to Christina rail against the idea of categorizing people.

For her part, Katie didn't share her friend's New Age ideas about the universe. Not one bit. She just thought contests like this were dumb. Beauty pageants, popularity contests, that sort of thing. Those kinds of contests didn't measure any skill. They were just a big festival of judging, and what was the point of that?

"Just tell them they can't do it," Christina said, winding to a close.

"I'd love to, but everything is supposed to be democratic. So if the majority wants a most popular, most beautiful, most likely to become a psychotic axe murderer—or whatever—page, then they get it," Katie said with an air of defeat.

It wasn't as though she hadn't tried to talk them out of it. She'd argued fiercely against it, but they were determined to have the contest. So, as editor, she put it to a vote, and she lost.

"But you're the editor," Christina protested. "You have the final word."

"Not quite. We voted," Katie said with philosophical resignation. "And we lost."

Katie and a girl named Sally Overton, who was editor of the school newspaper, were the only two against the idea. Christina obviously would have been with them, but she wasn't there.

The other kids on the staff said Katie and Sally were making too big a deal out of it. "Don't take it so seriously," a girl named Candy Martin scolded. "It's just fun." The rest agreed and insisted it was a Pine Ridge tradition to have a page of "mosts" and "bests."

"Darrin Tyson wanted to have a category called Worst Breath," Katie told Christina. "I told him no way on that one."

"Worst breath! You're kidding," Christina cried, aghast at the idea.

Katie rolled her amber eyes at the very thought. "Yeah, and get this. Rhonda Lynbrook wants to quit the yearbook staff so that she has a chance to be voted best looking. She doesn't want there to be any conflict of interest."

"Rhonda, best looking?" Christina shrieked in disbelief. "I know a lot of the boys like her . . . but best looking?"

"Didn't Rhonda tell you? Her mother was voted best looking when she went to Pine Ridge High. She's told everyone else on earth. She says she just has to follow in her mother's footsteps."

"Oh, another tradition. I don't believe it," Christina sighed dismally.

"Believe it." Katie laughed scornfully. "Who cares if she quits, anyway. She'll just want to put in a fashion section or something dweeby like that."

"Hang on a minute, okay?" Christina requested. "Someone's at the door. I think it's Ashley."

"Sure, go ahead."

A large black dog padded into the kitchen. "Dizzy," Katie said hopefully. "Bring me a soda, boy." She pointed to the small stack of cans by the fridge. "Bring soda. Fetch soda."

"Yes!" she cheered as the dog padded over to the cans and sniffed. Instead of a soda, though, he brought her a broken pencil that had fallen behind some of the cans. "Oh, well." She laughed, patting his head. "Nice try."

"Are you there, Katie?" Christina came back on the line.

"Yep."

"Ashley's here now. Why don't you come over to the ranch?"

"Did you call Molly?" Katie asked.

"Molly," Christina echoed with an unhappy sigh.

"What's the matter?" Katie asked. "Are you angry with Molly or something?"

"No. I'm worried that she might be angry with me when she finds out."

"Finds out what?"

Christina hesitated a moment before answering. "Matt's been calling me lately."

"Uh-oh," Katie said. She knew Christina had a huge crush on Molly's boyfriend, Matt Larson. She'd liked him before she was friends with Molly, but once the girls became friends, Christina had worked hard to put her feelings for Matt aside. "What's he calling for?" Katie asked.

"Just to talk," Christina answered.

"Has he asked you out?" Katie didn't waste time

being tactful. She always said exactly what was on her mind.

"No," Christina replied truthfully.

Katie thought a moment. It didn't seem fair to her. Molly wasn't all that interested in Matt. That much was clear, at least to Katie. "Molly won't care," she told Christina.

"Of course she will!" Christina cried. "I'm her friend and Matt is her boyfriend. I know she's going to be upset."

"Naw," Katie disagreed. "Whenever Molly has to choose between doing something with us or doing something with Matt, she comes with us. He's always the second choice. Besides, you and Matt have a lot in common, especially Children's House."

"Then why do I feel so guilty whenever I see her?" Christina questioned, unconvinced.

"Because you haven't told her about it," Katie offered bluntly. "Anyway, don't worry about it now. Her father comes back from Ireland today so she probably won't want to come."

"I'll call her anyway," Christina said. "I can't avoid her—that wouldn't be right. Are *you* coming over?"

Katie glanced at the round kitchen clock. "I don't know if I can get a ride. Aunt Rainie's still working at the hair salon and Uncle Jeff is out fixing somebody's tractor."

"What about Mel?" Christina asked.

"He's not here, either, but he usually shows up to eat around lunchtime. When he comes in, I'll ask him. I'll probably have to bribe him, but it's worth it."

"Good. Ashley wants to go to the Angel's Crossing Bridge. Want to go?"

"I thought you had a cold," Katie questioned.

"I do," Christina said, sniffing, as if to prove it. "Mom thought I was too sick to go to the meeting, but she's working now, and I don't really feel that bad anymore. I think I can talk her into letting me go for a walk."

"The bridge," Katie murmured thoughtfully. "Why does Ashley want to go there? Any special reason?"

"I don't think so," Christina replied. "We haven't been in a while."

"That's true." The idea of walking through the snowy woods to the bridge was appealing. Katie loved the bridge. And she never knew what would happen there, although something usually *did*.

"Are you sure something's not bothering Ashley?" Katie asked again. "Is the ranch in trouble?"

Ashley and Christina both lived at the Pine Manor Ranch, which Ashley's parents, Judy and Hank Kingsley, owned. Christina's mother, Alice, worked there as a trail guide, riding instructor, and ranch hand. The ranch, though gorgeous and fun, was often in financial difficulty. Winters were especially hard. There were times when there were no trail rides for weeks.

Katie wondered if that was why Ashley wanted to go to the bridge, to ask the angels for help. When one of them wanted to go to the bridge, it was usually for a special reason. The Angel's Crossing Bridge was buried deep in the Pine Manor woods. It was the place where they'd first encountered angels.

Christina lowered her voice. "She didn't tell me about

anything. It's been slow around here, but I guess that's because the weather has been so bad. I think she just feels like taking a walk out there. I wonder if we'll see . . . you know . . . them."

Katie *did* know who Christina was talking about.

Angels.

It had taken Katie a long time to accept the fact that she had actually seen angels. Her practical mind had searched for every possible logical explanation to challenge this fact. Once her brain had finally wrapped itself around the idea, Katie had come to believe that angels were indeed real and the bridge in the woods was a special place where they could be contacted. So much had happened, it was impossible to believe anything else.

"When Mel gets back, get him to give you a lift," Christina urged.

"All right, I'll try. I've got to go now. See you later." Katie hung up the phone and went to the fridge for her soda. As she flipped the pop-top, she gazed around the kitchen. It was the only new-looking room in the old house. That was thanks to Mel, who'd left a pot burning on the stove and set the old kitchen on fire. Even now the house still had a slightly smokey smell.

The new kitchen wasn't too bad, though. The cabinets were white and the shiny linoleum had a black-and-white stone pattern. The old kitchen had been so dingy and worn that Katie had found it depressing from the moment she saw it. Almost anything would have been an improvement.

With her usual horrible taste, Aunt Rainie had selected

a glossy wallpaper with yellow daisies, each daisy wearing a little smiling face at its center. Katie tried not to ever look at the wallpaper, but it was hard to avoid. The cheerful daisies were everywhere, their black eyes and maniacal grins impossible to ignore.

Leaving the kitchen, Katie went upstairs to her room with Dizzy trailing loyally behind her. Technically, he belonged to Mel. Since the fire, though, he'd adopted Katie as his owner. Katie was the one who'd taken care of Dizzy when the fireman carried him out of the burning kitchen, half-choked with smoke. She'd petted and soothed the frightened dog as the firemen worked to dampen the flames. It took guilty Mel more than a day to return and face up to what he had done. When he finally came back, Dizzy made it clear that he now belonged to Katie. Mel didn't seem to care, but Katie was glad to have a new friend.

Katie flopped onto her twin bed. The springs creaked, and her gray kitten, Nagle, scrambled off the edge where he'd been sleeping. She'd know when Mel came home because his motorcycle roared thunderously whenever it came down the rocky dirt drive that connected their house to the road.

Reaching between her mattress and box spring, Katie took out two notebooks. The black-and-white marble one was her private journal. The worn red spiral notebook held the short stories she was always writing.

Katie dreamed of being a writer and planned to someday be a journalist and travel around the world. Right now she wrote for the fun of it, with the hope that maybe one story would come out so well, she'd have the nerve to send it to a magazine or a publisher.

Looking at the two books, she decided to write in the journal first.

> *Why are people so quick to judge others? I don't understand it. What's the big rush to put everyone into a category? If you get voted Most Popular, what does it really do for you? What does it do for everyone who isn't voted Most Popular?*
>
> *Now that I'm writing about this I feel a little guilty. I wonder if I judged Aunt Rainie and Uncle Jeff when I first got here. It was so good of them to say I could live with them after Mom and Dad died. But I acted like they had done something horrible to me just because they're not as educated and comfortable as Mom and Dad were. That wasn't right.*
>
> *I didn't really know what to think when I first got here. I was still in shock, I guess, over Mom and Dad. Sometimes I still can't believe they're not here. But that's why I was so mean to everyone. I wanted my parents back, and I couldn't have that.*
>
> *I know now that Aunt Rainie and Uncle Jeff really care about me and that's what matters most. Maybe that's why I know how crazy it is to hang labels on people.*

Katie lifted her head and listened. A low rumble grew

ever louder outside. Going to the window, she gazed out at the sky crowded with thick gray clouds. Was it going to snow again, or would the snow clouds hang there like a threat for another day?

A lone figure on a motorcycle appeared, traveling toward the house. Dizzy jumped up beside her, his big black paws propped on the windowsill.

"I wish winter would end." She spoke to the dog. "I'm sick of it." The endless gray days depressed her.

Or was it the memory of the yearbook meeting that was getting her down? She felt so disillusioned with people lately. Every night Uncle Jeff watched the news, and there was always something awful. Some person had been cruel to someone else, some big company had polluted a bay, some unhappy group had bombed something. It made her feel very unhopeful about the state of the world. Why couldn't people get along with each other?

Maybe it was just being alone in the big, old, drafty, smoky-smelling house that was making her gloomy. "It's probably all that canned corned beef I ate." She chuckled darkly. The greasy food, Aunt Rainie's favorite "quick" meal, was settling like a rock in her stomach, as it always did.

Whatever the reason, the house suddenly seemed to press in on Katie, making her feel restless and dissatisfied with everything. She longed to get out and search for something wonderful, something that would lift her spirits.

She longed to see the angels.

Would Mel be willing to take her to the ranch? She

hoped so. "Come on, Diz," she said, turning away from
the window. "Let's go see Mel before he takes his helmet
off. Once he settles in front of the TV to watch the stock
car races, there's not a chance of him going out there
into the cold again."

3

Mr. Morgan had barely slipped into the booth beside Molly when she began bombarding him with questions. "Who is he, Dad? Why is he here?"

Her father settled into his seat and sighed wearily. The trip home had obviously tired him. "As I said, Liam's the son of my childhood pal Conor McDermott," he began, resting his hands on the table and pressing his fingertips together thoughtfully. "Liam looks exactly like Conor did when he was that age, in fact."

"Have you kept in touch with him all these years?" Molly asked. She didn't remember her father ever mentioning the man.

"No. Not at all. I was down by the beach painting one morning when who should come strolling down the strand but Conor himself." Mr. Morgan smiled at the happy memory.

"How odd," Molly noted, "to just run into him like that after so many years."

"Not as odd as it sounds," Mr. Morgan replied. "In

Ireland, people often stay put, living in one town their entire lives. And it was on that very same beach that I first met Conor as a boy."

Molly remembered the rocky shore of that beach well. She'd seen it for the first time several months ago when she'd visited her family's ancient castle in Ireland. The beach and dark, churning ocean were at the bottom of a craggy cliff. The towering castle sat atop a high peak from which one could gaze down at the water below.

"We were glad to see one another," her father continued. "We talked for ages, trying to catch up on each other's lives. We arranged for Conor to come for lunch at the castle the next day, which he did. But he didn't come alone—Liam was with him."

"What's the matter with Liam?" Molly asked.

Mr. Morgan sighed again. "Hard to say, exactly. What Conor told me is this: Liam went out horseback riding one afternoon with his best friend, Brian. The two boys brought the horses up to the top of one of the cliffs overlooking the beach when—"

"Excuse me," Joy interrupted, stepping into the breakfast nook with a cordless phone in her hand. "Phone for you, Molly."

Molly growled in frustration. Why did someone have to call now? "Do you know who it is, Joy?" she asked impatiently.

Joy shook her head. "It's a boy."

"Better take it," her father teased.

"Oh, it's probably just Matt," Molly told him, easing herself out of the booth. "I'll be right back. Don't go away. I have to hear the rest of this story."

Molly went into the large formal dining room and pulled out a smooth polished chair. Clicking off the hold button, she put the phone to her ear. "Matt?"

"Hi, Molly." The tone of his voice made her frown with concern. He sounded so uncomfortable. She'd gone steady with Matt Larson since the beginning of seventh grade. Now they were in the eighth. Why was he so ill at ease with her all of a sudden? Molly got the feeling he was hiding something, but whenever she tried to talk to him about it, he changed the subject.

"Is everything all right?" she asked. "You sound weird."

He cleared his throat. "Oh, do I? Sorry." After an awkward pause, he began again. "Listen, Molly, I need to talk to you. It's kind of important. Will you be home for a while?"

A line of goosebumps spread up Molly's spine. What had happened? What could be so important? From the sound of his voice, Molly knew it wasn't something good. "Can't you tell me right now?" she asked.

"I'd rather talk to you in person. Can I come right over?"

"Yes, sure."

"Okay. I'll be there in a few minutes. Bye."

Molly clicked off as her mind raced with possibilities. What would he have to say?

Maybe he'd been grounded for doing so badly in algebra this quarter. Did that mean he wouldn't be able to take her to the Valentine's Dance? Molly hoped that wasn't it. She'd been looking forward to the dance, and she'd finally found the perfect dress.

Matt lived only a few blocks away. He'd be over soon, and then she'd find out what the mystery was. There was no point in sitting there guessing. She'd hear the bad news soon enough.

Hurrying back to the breakfast nook, she slipped into the booth next to her father. "Go on," she prompted. "Liam and Brian were on top of a cliff with the horses. Then what?"

"Well, a storm came up suddenly, a terrible storm. Brian's horse became terrified at the thunder and lightning. She reared again and again, and then lost her footing."

Molly's hands flew to her cheeks. She could picture those cliffs looming above the ocean, so jagged, rocky, and steep. "How horrible!" she sympathized. "Was he hurt?"

"Yes." Mr. Morgan paused, collecting his thoughts. "Brian's horse crashed over the side of the cliff and landed on the beach."

Molly gasped. "And Brian?"

Mr. Morgan nodded darkly. "He didn't make it. He and the horse were found on the beach, dead."

"Oh, no! How sad! What about Liam?"

"Liam's horse also panicked and threw the boy, but in the opposite direction, away from the cliff's edge. It wasn't until after dark that the search party found Liam lying unconscious against a rock with his head split open."

"Oh, my gosh," Molly murmured, picturing the awful scene. "Poor Liam."

Mr. Morgan nodded. "They rushed him to the hospital,

and he remained in a coma for two days. Even after he came out of it, Conor said, things were touch and go for several more days. They didn't know if he would make it at all."

"But he did," Molly interjected. "He's not all right, though, is he?"

Mr. Morgan shook his head. "Conor said that Liam seemed to improve pretty rapidly until they told him about Brian's death."

"And then . . ." Molly prodded.

Her father smiled sadly. "He retreated into a shell. Now he can't—or won't—speak."

"Joy said he seemed in shock," Molly offered.

Mr. Morgan's face twisted thoughtfully as he considered this. "Not shock. Not exactly, but close. The doctors called it a semicatatonic state. Physically, he sees and hears, but he doesn't respond. They don't know if things are making sense to him, if he's comprehending them or not. They don't know if he *can't* respond or if, for some reason, he's choosing not to."

"That's terrible," Molly sympathized. "But why did you bring him here?"

Sitting back in the booth, Mr. Morgan folded his arms. "It was a funny thing. Conor and I spent a lot of time together. One day he brought Liam to the painting studio I had set up at the old caretaker's cottage. They watched me paint, and Conor said that Liam seemed more alert than he had in months. His eyes grew bright, and he studied every move I made. He seemed to want to say something, although he didn't. In a way, he seemed very agitated."

"Agitated?" Molly questioned.

"Yes. As if watching me paint was bothering him, upsetting him."

"So you brought him here to be more bothered?" Molly questioned skeptically. "I don't understand how that can be good for him."

"His doctors said that any reaction, even agitation, is better than no reaction. Being agitated is like working a muscle, an emotional muscle. If he's upset, he has a better chance of coming out of his buried emotional state."

"I get it," Molly said. "Being upset showed that he was aware of things outside himself."

"Right. Exactly. So Liam's father and I decided that he should come with me and watch me paint some more. I called Mom and discussed it with her, and she agreed. I asked her not to mention anything to you or Joy because I wanted Liam's arrival to be as quiet as possible. He's been through so many changes, I thought it might be too much for him to be greeted by a welcoming committee when he arrived." Mr. Morgan looked into his daughter's eyes. "Perhaps those words he wants to speak will finally burst forth."

"What do you think gets him so worked up?" Molly asked. "Does he hate your paintings or something?"

"I don't know. I hope they're not *that* bad," Mr. Morgan replied with a wry smile. "I thought I might take him to see Dr. Andrews, a friend of mine who's a psychiatrist. He might be able to shed some light on Liam's condition. It couldn't hurt."

The front doorbell rang. Molly knew it had to be

Matt. "I wonder if there really is a way to get through to him," Molly puzzled out loud as she left the kitchen nook.

She reached the front door still thinking about Liam. She pictured his horrible accident and imagined how awful he must have felt when he learned his friend had died.

But as soon as she touched the shiny brass doorknob to open the door, all thoughts of Liam flew out of her mind. In minutes she'd hear what Matt had to say. What could be so terrible that he couldn't tell her over the phone?

Letting out a quick, fluttering breath, she opened the door. Before her stood a tall, broad-shouldered boy with longish, sandy-colored hair. He had handsome features and expressive blue eyes behind wire-rim glasses. His face was so familiar to Molly that she no longer really noticed his good looks.

What she *did* notice was the stricken expression on his face. Matt looked as if the world were coming to an end.

"You're moving," she guessed, the idea suddenly hitting her. "That's it, isn't it?" What else could possibly make him this unhappy?

"I wish it were that simple, Molly," he said, shaking his head dismally.

4

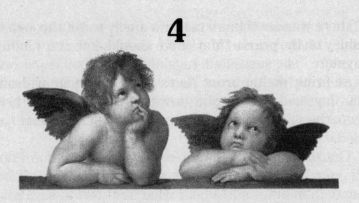

Christina peered down the long drive separating the Pine Manor Ranch from the roadway. Her sky-blue eyes narrowed slightly as she tried to see all the way to the end. A blast of cold wind kicked up a spray of snow, sailing it across the newly plowed drive.

Some of that snow drifted into the collar of Christina's heavy quilted winter jacket. Shivering, she stuffed her thick, wavy wheat-colored hair into the collar. From her jacket pocket she pulled a large purple cotton scarf covered with a silver and gold pattern of the moon and stars and tied it around her neck.

A door slammed. Christina turned to see a petite redhead in a heavy gold woolen jacket coming out of the yellow ranch-style house. She stopped a moment on the sheltered front porch and produced a gold woolen headband from her pocket. Flipping back her mane of wild curls, Ashley pulled on the headband, setting it in place at the top of her forehead. "Is she coming?" she called to Christina.

"I don't see her car," Christina replied.

There was another slam of the door, and Katie joined Ashley on the porch. "Maybe we shouldn't wait for Molly anymore," she suggested, tugging her baseball cap down more firmly on her brow. "Let's go to the bridge without her. Joy said she'd gone down to the pond on their property with Matt. They probably went skating or something."

"But she told Joy she would be right back," Ashley disagreed. "I told Joy to tell her we'd be going to the bridge. She always likes to come. Let's wait just a few more minutes."

Christina started to walk toward the horse stable just across from Ashley's house. The snow crunched crisply beneath her boots.

"Where are you going?" Ashley called to her.

"Just over here. The stable is warm," Christina called back. The truth, though, was that she didn't want her friends to see her face. She feared her expression might reveal her true feelings for Matt. The image of Molly and Matt together, probably holding hands as they walked in the silent winter landscape, made her so jealous she could hardly conceal it.

Not that they didn't know about her huge crush on Matt. They knew. But Christina had convinced them—or was pretty sure she had—that she was over it. She couldn't think of liking Matt. Not in *that* way. It would be wrong, much too disloyal to Molly to even consider.

Yet, secretly, she liked him more than ever. Like Christina and Katie, Matt worked as a volunteer at Children's House, a special, homey pediatric facility on the grounds of the larger, more austere Pine Ridge

Hospital. They helped the sick children there, talking with them, doing fun activities. Matt was so good with the kids, especially the boys.

Their work at the hospital often threw Matt and Christina together. When she was with him, Christina felt she could talk to him about the things that truly mattered to her—her beliefs in spirituality, the occult, the power of energy. And about angels.

Matt believed in angels, too.

Christina hadn't ever revealed to him all the details of her encounters with angels. But it wasn't out of embarrassment or lack of trust. It was because the girls had agreed to keep quiet about the angels on the bridge. They didn't want to draw attention to it, fearing that the woods would become spoiled with curiosity seekers.

Still, she could have told Matt. He was open to things like that, although his real interest was outer space. Nonetheless, he didn't make fun of her beliefs, like so many of the boys Christina knew from school. Matt would take in her secret and keep it to himself.

Christina pushed her weight into the heavy stable door and slowly opened it. Immediately, the warm, moist smell of horses enveloped her. Soft nickers protested the blast of cold she'd let into the horses' comfortable domain, and she pushed the door shut again. "Sorry," she told the shifting, curious horses who gazed at her over their stalls.

Christina pressed her gloved fingers against the small white scar that crossed her left eyebrow. The skin around it always ached a little when the weather turned really cold. Warming it with her glove instantly removed the ache.

What made this whole Matt thing worse was that Christina felt so guilty. The moment she became friendly with Molly, she'd tried to back away from Matt. She was careful never to be too friendly. Just friendly enough to be nice.

Yet, last night she hadn't been able to resist laying out the tarot cards on her bed. Christina wholeheartedly believed that the cards could predict the future. She asked the cards if she had a chance with Matt. Her reply came in the form of the fortune card. It meant good luck. She'd have good luck with Matt.

What exactly did that mean?

Did it mean he'd break up with Molly and ask Christina out?

The very thought had made Christina gasp with happiness and then frown deeply. Would that really be good luck? How could she ever enjoy her good luck if it meant Molly's bad luck?

Maybe it meant that her good luck would be that Matt would never give her a second glance. Then, she'd be lucky enough to keep her close friend.

Not wanting to think about it anymore, she'd restacked the cards and quickly put them back in her dresser drawer.

From a nearby stall, Bridey, Christina's favorite mare, whinnied, as if calling to Christina. Going into the stall, she removed her glove and ran her hand along the horse's brown-and-white-spotted side. "Did you ever have a secret love, Bridey?" she sadly asked the horse.

Bridey nodded her head emphatically, which made Christina laugh. Did Bridey really understand the question? How could she? And yet, maybe it was possible. It seemed to Christina that horses possessed an awesome, even mystical, understanding of what went on around them.

The door opened, and in walked Ashley and Katie with Molly. She hadn't even heard a car pull up, but then the sleek, purring cars that transported Molly to and fro never made much noise. They certainly didn't rattle and groan to announce their arrival the way Christina's mother's old brown pickup truck did.

One look at Molly's expression told Christina that something was terribly wrong. The girl's delicate brow was creased into a scowl. The rims of her eyes were red, as if she'd been crying.

"Molly, what happened?" Christina demanded, rushing toward her.

"It's Matt," Molly revealed, her lower lip shaking as she spoke.

"What happened to him?" Christina asked urgently.

Ashley shot her a disapproving look.

What's going on? Christina wondered.

"He's fine!" Molly blurted. "He broke up with me!"

Christina clapped her hands over her mouth in horror. The image of the fortune card filled her head. Had the tarot's prediction come true?

Christina, who always strove to be truthful, who held the truth in the highest esteem, couldn't stand to be hypocritical now. She spun away from them, so that only the horses could see her conflicted expression. She was truly sorry for Molly's pain. Yet Matt was free now. Did she have a chance with him?

"Are you all right, Christina?" Katie asked knowingly.

"Oh, uh, yeah," Christina stammered.

Silently, she scolded herself. *You're awful to think about dating Matt. The breakup just happened, and you want to know how fast you can take Molly's place.*

She couldn't help it, though. Her mind wouldn't stop racing with the possibilities this new development opened to her. Did he like her? Should she make the first move and ask him out? She could invite him to the movies at the mall. But what if he said no?

Stop! she demanded of herself. *Think about your friend. Molly must feel so bad right now.*

Forcing herself to turn back around, she saw that Ashley had put her arm comfortingly around Molly's slim shoulders. "Did he say why he wanted to break up?" Ashley inquired in a kind voice.

Molly nodded, despondently kicking the lose straw on the ground with the toe of her polished boot as she spoke. "He said we just weren't as close as we used to be. He doesn't feel that I really consider him a close friend." Seeming on the brink of tears, she tugged at the hem of her jacket. When she was more in control, she spoke again. "Before he left, he admitted the real reason," she said in a pain-filled voice.

"What . . . what is that?" Christina dared to ask.

Molly raised her head sharply. "He likes someone else better than he likes me," she confessed.

"Oh, she's probably some real jerk," Katie jumped in. "Some stupid, dumb twerp."

"No," Molly disagreed. "Matt wouldn't go for someone like that."

"Sure, he would," Katie insisted. "Nice, cute guys are always asking out the most unbelievably awful girls."

"That's true," Ashley agreed. "She's probably horrible. You know how boys are."

While Katie and Ashley went on deriding this new girl in Matt's life, Christina pulled in a long breath of horse-scented air to steady herself. Who was this other girl? Was she, Christina, the one, or was it someone else?

She quickly realized what a terrible position she was in. If Matt already liked someone new, she probably didn't stand a chance with him. He liked this new girl so much that he'd gone and broken up with Molly. He had to feel serious about her.

On the other hand, if she was the one, if the dream she'd held for all these months was finally coming true, then she was in an even worse position. Molly would hate her. Her friends might blame her for the breakup, too.

She couldn't possibly say yes to Matt if he asked her out. But how could she say no? The very thought of brushing him off made her stomach ache.

"Come on, Molly," Ashley said gently. "Let's go to the bridge. It's good that we were going. I think you could really use a visit with the angels right now."

With tender solicitude, Katie and Ashley led Molly from the stable. Christina followed.

"Molly's not the only one who could use a trip to the bridge," she muttered shakily as she pushed her shoulder against the stable door, sliding it shut.

5

Ashley's green eyes moved from one friend to the next as they made their way through the silent, snowy Pine Manor woods. She watched all three, but especially Christina and Molly, looking for signs that would tell her how they were really feeling. She had so many questions that she couldn't come out and ask.

Did Molly know how Christina felt about Matt? How was Christina taking the news of Molly and Matt's breakup? Would this breakup affect Molly's anorexia? Would it set her back and make her begin starving herself once again? Were Molly and Christina headed for a big blow-up?

Ashley felt as bad for Christina as she did for Molly. Maybe even worse for Christina. After all, she and Christina were like sisters. They'd grown up together on the ranch ever since they were both five and Christina's mother had come to work for Ashley's parents. They had been through a lot together, and Christina was always there for her.

She knew people thought they didn't seem to have much in common other than their both being the same age and living on the ranch. People saw Christina as wild and imaginative, maybe a little flaky. Ashley was the sensible girl. Pretty, neat, down to earth.

But there was more to her. And more to Christina. Ashley didn't really care what people thought. She loved Christina like a sister, and that was all there was to it.

Now, as they all walked without speaking, each privately listening to the thunderous silence of the ancient, towering woods, Ashley imagined she had some idea of how Christina must be feeling.

Awful.

She knew how crazy Christina was about Matt. Even though she denied it, Ashley wasn't blind. She saw how Christina's expressive eyes lit up whenever Matt was around.

Ashley also knew what an honest, kind person her friend was. Christina liked Molly a lot and would never want to hurt her.

But *would* she be hurting Molly? Really?

She glanced at Molly, trudging along despondently, head down against the wind that whistled past the thick, weathered trunks of the pines. Sure, she felt bad. Nobody liked to be dumped.

But Ashley wondered how much Molly really cared about Matt. Down deep. Once she'd been confident of his devotion, Molly hadn't paid all that much attention to him. It appeared to Ashley that Molly took Matt for granted.

They'd broken up once before. But when Molly's

anorexia grew worse and she had to be hospitalized, faithful Matt had been at her side. His loyalty had helped Molly combat the deadly disease.

Katie caught Ashley's eye and shot her a perplexed look. Ashley rolled her eyes as a sort of reply. Katie was probably thinking similar thoughts about Christina and Molly. Did Katie hate being in the middle as much as Ashley did? Probably, Ashley decided.

They continued walking, and Ashley's thoughts drifted. She began thinking about the ranch. This morning she'd overheard her parents discussing their finances. Her father said this had been their worst winter yet. If things didn't pick up soon, they might have to sell some of the horses to cover expenses.

Winter was always a hard time at the ranch. There were fewer trail rides, and the inn was closed for the season. Ashley's parents had to stretch the money they'd made during the nice weather over the long, cold winter. Ashley hated that her parents' money worries seemed endless. They worked so hard and tried so many different things, but they always seemed to come up short.

Ashley had heard her mother say that her older twin brothers, Jeremy and Jason, might never get to college at this rate. There was no way they could ever afford to send the boys. Ashley had groaned inwardly. She had always dreamed of going away to college. Now it appeared her dream would never come true. If only there was something she could do to help them all.

After a while the girls came to a narrow running stream. "I wonder why it's not frozen?" Ashley puzzled, gazing down at the crystal-clear water as it danced over stones in its path.

"Because it's moving, maybe," Katie speculated.

They followed the little stream as they always did when they were heading for the Angel's Crossing Bridge. The Pine Manor woods was vast, and it was easy to get lost. The girls had long ago established landmarks, like this stream, that always helped lead them safely to the bridge.

As they walked quietly along the side of the stream, Molly lifted her head and began telling the others about Liam.

"I'll give you lavender crystals for him," Christina volunteered after Molly finished her story.

Katie groaned loudly. "What, exactly, is that going to do for the poor guy?" she asked in the same impatient tone she always used when talking to Christina about this sort of thing.

Ashley shook her head and laughed silently. Katie had always been practical, and she had no patience with Christina's New Age beliefs.

"Crystals are energy conductors," Christina explained with exaggerated patience, as if she were talking to a five-year-old. She'd been over this with Katie a million times. "Crystals help focus energy."

"What kind of energy?" Katie challenged. "Electric energy? Solar energy? What?"

"Cosmic energy," Christina replied. "The energy of the universe."

"How do you know there's such a thing as cosmic energy?" Katie shot back.

"Because I know," Christina insisted. "You can't see other forms of energy, but they're there. And we know there are forces in the world we can't see."

"I don't know that," Katie said stubbornly.

Christina stared hard and meaningfully at her. "Yes, you do. We all do. What about the angels?"

"All right. So there are angels. I know that because I can see them. But just because angels exist doesn't mean there's such a thing as cosmic energy," Katie countered. "They're not the same thing."

"Please don't argue, we're almost at the bridge," Ashley cut in. She always played the role of peacemaker, but she didn't mind. With two older brothers, it was a skill that came naturally to her. She liked everyone to get along and be happy.

"We weren't fighting. We were having a debate on the nature of the universe," Katie told Ashley, her amber eyes sparkling merrily.

"Oh," Ashley said, smiling. "I didn't realize."

"No, I didn't realize, either," Molly played along.

Christina shook her head and rolled her eyes. "Neither did I."

The four girls stopped at a spot where the stream disappeared into the side of a hill, and they gazed up. Drifts of snow had settled between the trees that dotted the hillside. It wouldn't be easy to climb, but they started up anyway.

Ashley found herself breathing heavily by the time they reached the top. Leaning forward, panting, her heart pounding from the effort, she surveyed the tranquil scene before her. No matter how many times Ashley saw it, she was always filled with a sense of awe and peace.

At the bottom of the hill sat an old covered wooden bridge, open halfway up the sides. The thick trees parted above it, letting shafts of yellow-white winter light filter down softly and shine gently on the broken wooden shingles of the bridge's slightly sagging roof.

The weatherbeaten bridge once led to the old manor house that now lay in ruins on the far side of it. This woods was named after the once grand Pine Manor. Whatever road had led to and from the bridge had long ago been reclaimed by the woods, and the bridge had fallen into disrepair.

Below the bridge a foaming, crashing creek rushed by, throwing up jets of white spray as it leaped over small rock ledges in its frantic race to some unknown destination. In winter, surrounded by snow and blocked here and there by bare, fallen branches that had tumbled across its path, the creek seemed more clear, sparkling, and alive than ever.

Yet, it wasn't the beauty of the creek or the dignified stillness of the aged bridge that awed Ashley. Rather, it was her knowledge of what this place really was that affected her so deeply. It was a special place where angels crossed easily from their spiritual world to this world.

Christina called it a power spot, meaning a place where positive energy pooled and drew all good things to it. Ashley wasn't sure about that. It was possible, she supposed. All she knew was that they'd first met the angels here.

"Let's go," Katie said, heading down the hill first.

Ashley, Molly, and Christina followed close behind. Together, they stepped onto the creaking wooden planks of the bridge.

"I don't see anyone," Katie noted dismally as she checked either side of the bridge.

Ashley felt disappointment wash over her. "Oh, well, it was a nice walk," she said, trying to be positive.

"A waste of time, you mean," Molly said sourly. "And it's cold."

Christina gazed out over the creek, seemingly lost in her own very private thoughts.

Ashley absently pulled off her black fleece gloves, then loosened the top button of her jacket. "Is anyone else warm all of a sudden?" she asked, realizing she was growing uncomfortable under all her layers of clothing.

"You're right," Katie remarked, tugging at her collar. "It is warm."

"Well, we're sheltered under this roof," Molly suggested, searching for an explanation.

"What's that?" asked Christina as she looked up sharply. "Do you hear something?"

"I do," Katie confirmed. "It's . . . it's music."

"Strange music," Molly added.

The music grew louder. It wasn't modern music, not rock or pop or jazz. It wasn't classical music, either. "What kind of music is that?" Ashley asked, straining to remember where she'd heard it before. Odd as it was, the music was also strangely familiar.

"Egypt!" Katie cried.

"You're right," Christina agreed, untying her purple scarf and lifting her flowing blonde hair from inside her collar. "That music sounds like it's from ancient Egypt." She wiped her forehead with the back of her hand. "Wow! It's really hot now!"

A strong wind suddenly whipped through the bridge. A warm wind! It tossed their hair and flung their scarves into the air.

Ashley's hands flew to her face as something scratchy brushed across her cheeks.

Sand!

6

Sensing a new presence nearby, Molly spun around to face the tumult of hot wind. "Oh!" The gasp escaped her lips before she realized she was speaking.

Three tall, majestic figures stood at the far end of the dilapidated bridge. They seemed strangely illuminated, as though a light shone behind them. Or was it coming *from* them?

In the middle of the trio stood a man wearing a strange golden headpiece. It came straight up and was square on top. He wore no shirt, but across his chest was a gleaming golden breastplate etched with a beautiful design. He wore a straight white skirt that fell just below his knees, and golden sandals on his feet.

A woman stood on either side of him. One had flowing golden curls covered by a threadbare scarf. She wore a dull brown-gray tunic, and she looked like a peasant. The other woman had straight, silken black hair cut blunt across the bottom. She was dressed in a crisp white tunic that was clasped across one shoulder with a golden pin in the shape of a snake. Golden snake bracelets coiled around her upper arms. This woman looked like a queen.

Molly smiled radiantly. She knew them all.

Ned, Norma, and Edwina were the angels the girls most frequently encountered on the bridge. At first, they hadn't been sure the three even were angels. Katie had believed they were just three eccentric people who lived in the woods and liked to hang out by the bridge. But after a while there could be no doubt the three were angels. They had admitted as much, and the girls had been helped so often by this unlikely trio that they knew it was true.

"Why are you dressed like that?" Christina blurted. Of all the girls, Christina was the least astounded by the angels. She was the one most at ease with them, maybe because she'd believed in angels her whole life.

Ned stepped forward, lifting the heavy headpiece off his head and rolling the kinks out of his neck. "Now I know where the expression 'pain in the neck' came from," he said, eyeing the headpiece distastefully. "This thing weighs a ton."

"We were in ancient Egypt," Edwina, the delicate-featured blonde, told them.

"Angels in ancient Egypt?" Katie cried, astonished.

Edwina laughed melodically. "Sure, why not? The first people to write about angels were in ancient Persia. They were the Zoroastrians. But you hear about us in ancient writings of all kinds. We've been around for a long time."

"You mean the same angels who were around then are around now?" Katie questioned.

"We've been around forever," Norma, the black-haired woman, replied.

"Time isn't the same for a spirit as it is for a physical body," Ned added. "It's really hard to explain. I still don't fully understand it myself."

"Why did they need you in ancient Egypt?" Christina asked.

"Oh, you wouldn't believe what a terrible time the poor slaves are having in Egypt," Edwina said, frowning sadly. "Building those pyramids in the hot sun! Unbelievable!" She shook her head wearily. "Those poor people needed all the help I could give them. If I hadn't lifted those stones for one dear old man, I'm sure he'd have collapsed and never gotten up."

Molly recalled pictures of the pyramids she had seen in her history book. She remembered a drawing of slaves bent under the immense stones as they hauled them into place to build the awesome triangular tombs for the pharaohs. Forevermore, she'd envision a winged angel helping to lift those stones whenever she thought of the pyramids.

"It's not so easy being a princess, either," said Norma. As she came closer, Molly noticed the black eyeliner rimming her strange, lavender-blue, almond-shaped eyes. All three angels had the same amazing eye color.

"Do you know they wanted that poor young girl to be shut up in the pyramid with her dead husband, the pharaoh? Buried alive! And she was only fifteen. The boy was only sixteen himself, and it was a shame he died, but the girl didn't deserve such a fate. I had a tough time getting her out of that one, let me tell you!" Norma exclaimed.

Molly remembered the mummies she'd seen in the museum. She'd seen one mummy of a young pharaoh who was only sixteen when he died. She wondered if this could be the same one.

"How did you get her out of it?" Christina asked eagerly.

Norma perched on the side railing of the bridge and pulled off a pair of golden sandals, wriggling her toes as though she were glad to be rid of them. "Oh, well, it was easy for me to look enough like her to enter the pyramid in her place. But then I had the problem of what to do with the girl. I didn't know how I was going to sneak her out of the palace. At the last minute, though, she surprised me by slipping away from her servants and blending in with the slaves."

"You mean, you can be surprised by what people do?" Katie inquired thoughtfully.

Ned laughed. "Are you kidding? We're surprised by people all the time. Completely freaked out, as you kids say."

"They don't say that anymore," Edwina told him drolly.

Ned rubbed his chin. "They don't?"

"No, that's from the late nineteen sixties, early nineteen seventies," Norma informed him. "We're years ahead of that."

Ned sighed. "This moving around in time can get confusing."

"Tell me about it." Edwina laughed, yanking the scarf from her head and freeing her thick mane of blonde curls.

Ned turned his attention back to Molly. "At any rate, people are constantly confounding us."

"You mean, we always have a choice about what we do?" she asked.

"Always," Ned confirmed.

"Take this Egyptian princess, for instance," Norma said. "She made the decision to slip in among the slaves. All I really did was keep the others from searching for her and dragging her back. They thought I was the princess, and they saw me follow the young pharaoh's sarcophagus into the pyramid tomb chamber. So everything worked out for the best."

"That young girl was doing a lot of good among the slaves," Edwina put in. "She was comforting the older workers and tending to the children. She also has an education. Just before I left, she was teaching a young man how to write and read hieroglyphics. She seemed very happy."

"But she'll be a slave all her life," Ashley said, feeling worried for the princess, as if she knew her.

"Not all her life," Ned assured her. "Pretty soon things will happen that will force the new pharaoh to let the slaves go."

"You guys sure lead interesting lives," Christina commented.

"It *is* interesting," Edwina admitted.

"Is there anything in particular we can do for you young ladies?" Ned asked. "We came back to this time because we felt you needed us."

Molly blinked hard at him. He no longer wore his exotic Egyptian outfit. Somehow he'd switched into a pair of bright white sweats with matching running sneakers.

The girls looked at one another, but no one spoke.

"Maybe your concerns are personal. Close your eyes and think about what you most need," Edwina suggested.

7

The four girls closed their eyes and thought their special, private thoughts.

Ashley had two concerns. *I need to find a way to help my parents keep the ranch going.* She spoke the words silently in her mind. *If the ranch made more money, then Jeremy and Jason could go to college next fall and we wouldn't have to sell any of the horses.*

Katie was still thinking about the popularity contest in the school yearbook and was still bothered by it. *I wish I understood people better. They seem so petty and small-minded to me. I'm afraid I'm growing to dislike people in general. But I don't want to feel that way. I want to see the good in people. How do I find it?*

Molly squeezed her eyes tightly. *Why doesn't Matt like me anymore? I need to know. I need to find out what I did wrong and how I can fix it. That's all—Oh . . . One more thing. I'd also like to find a way to help Liam if that's possible. I feel so sorry for him.*

Christina covered her face with her hands. *I'm not*

*sure how to express this. I want two things. I'd like
Matt to ask me out, but I don't want to hurt Molly. Is
there a way both things can happen? And, as long as
you're asking, I'll make one more request. Lately I've
been wondering about the things I believe. I think
Katie's doubt is finally getting to me. Is there really
cosmic energy? Can the future be told? Do crystals
work? Or is it all in my imagination, the way Katie
says? I'd like some kind of sign so I know whether or
not I should believe these things. Thanks.*

"We've heard you all. You can open your eyes now."
Edwina's voice came to them as a whisper.

The girls opened their eyes and gazed around,
bewildered.

The angels had vanished.

"Where'd they go?" Katie asked.

"I don't know," said Molly, "but it's suddenly gotten
cold again."

Moving fast, the girls began rewrapping themselves
with their scarves and gloves, zipping up their jackets
against the chill.

"They could have said good-bye," Katie grumbled.

"Maybe they had an emergency," Christina suggested.
"You know how it is with angels."

"Look!" Ashley cried, pointing at the fat snowflakes
that had begun to fall. "How beautiful!"

Christina stretched out her hand, capturing several
flakes on her glove. "Isn't it amazing that every one of
them is different?" she considered, studying the well-
formed flakes in her hand.

"How does anyone really know that?" Katie wondered,

reaching over the side of the bridge and capturing her own snowflakes. "I mean, they melt so fast, and who's ever seen every snowflake?"

"I don't know," Ashley said. "But scientists say it's true."

"It's true about fingerprints," Molly added. "No two people have the same prints. So why can't it be true of snowflakes?"

Christina continued inspecting her snowflakes as they slowly disappeared into her glove. She was glad Katie doubted something scientists said was true. Everything that didn't make sense to Katie wasn't necessarily untrue. She wondered if the angels had answered her request already. Was this their way of telling her not to let Katie's doubts overwhelm her? Maybe.

"We'd better get back," Ashley suggested. "This snow looks like it's going to keep coming. We don't want to be caught out here in a blizzard."

Knowing Ashley was right, the girls left the bridge and began the return trip to the ranch, retracing the familiar path they'd walked into the woods. Once they were under the protection of the dense pine canopy, the snow stopped falling on them as furiously as it had by the creek. Just a light haze of snow filtered down through the thick branch covering, dusting them gently as they walked. Along the way, Katie stopped to pick up some large pinecones that dotted her path.

"What will you do with them?" Ashley asked.

"I don't know exactly," Katie admitted with a shrug as she stuffed them into her jacket pockets. "Maybe we can do a craft project with the kids at Children's House."

"Good idea," Christina agreed. She bent down and started to collect more pinecones.

When they emerged from the woods, the girls were amazed at how intense the storm had become.

With a welcoming bark, Champ, Ashley's golden retriever, bounded off the front porch. "He loves the snow," Ashley said, laughing. She scooped up a snowball and hurled it high into the air.

Champ leaped up and caught the snowball, which exploded in his jaws. The comical sight made the girls laugh.

Immediately, they launched into an all-out snowball fight in front of the stable. Laughing and hurling snowballs, they fought their way down the slippery drive. To escape being hit, Katie ducked through the bottom opening in one of the split rail fences that surrounded the huge grazing pasture on the right side of the drive. Her friends chased her, enjoying kicking up a path through the pristine, unmarked snow.

Finally, breathless from laughing, running, throwing, and ducking, the girls stood panting in the middle of the field. "Let's make a snowman," Ashley suggested as soon as her breathing slowed to normal.

In less than twenty minutes they'd constructed a form about five feet tall. Pulling off her purple scarf with the cosmic design, Christina wrapped it around the figure's neck. Katie took some pinecones from her pocket and made rows of them on the snow figure's head for hair. "I can always go back to the woods to get more for the craft project," she commented. Christina added the cones she'd collected, and soon the figure had a fine head of pinecone hair.

"That hairdo makes it looks more like a she than a he," Molly commented.

"Okay, so it's a snowwoman," Katie said. "Why not?"

Christina began packing snow onto the figure's right shoulder blade. It soon became obvious she was forming a wing. "A snow angel. Cool!" Ashley exclaimed. She scooped up a handful of snow and began working on the left shoulder blade. When the wings reached a certain size, they began crumbling, refusing to grow any larger.

"Not exactly great wings," Christina admitted.

"Oh, well," Ashley said, shrugging. "We tried." A shiver ran through her. She looked down and realized her jeans were soaked through.

"Hey, I have an idea," Christina said. "Let's go back to my house for hot chocolate."

"Excellent idea," Katie agreed enthusiastically.

They ran back across the pasture and out to the drive. It didn't take long to reach the rustic cabin just off the drive where Christina and her mother lived. A cozy fire burning in the stone fireplace greeted them as they walked in. "Oh, this is nice," Molly cooed, moving to the fire to warm her hands.

Christina's mother, a tall woman with short blonde hair, came into the living room dressed in a heavy jacket and boots. "Oh, good, Christina, you're here," Alice said with a smile. "Now I won't have to put out the fire."

Christina stepped into the small kitchen, which was separated from the living room by a long counter. "Where are you going?" she asked her mother.

"Over to the stable. I want to give the horses extra hay

in their stalls. This storm is supposed to get worse, and I want them to stay warm."

"Do you need help?" Christina offered.

"No, thanks, honey. It's been so quiet around here lately, I'm glad to have something to do," her mother replied. She left, and Christina took a half-gallon container of milk from the refrigerator.

As she poured some into a pot, the phone on the kitchen wall rang. "Could someone get that?" Christina asked as she struggled with the milk.

Molly headed for the phone. "I bet it's my mother wanting me to come home," she guessed. "I was so upset about Matt that I went out without my cellular."

Katie laughed. "So that's what's missing!" she teased. "I knew you looked different today." Molly rarely traveled without the small leather bag that contained her cellular phone. It had been a gift from her parents for her thirteenth birthday.

"Hello," Molly answered the phone.

"Hi, Christina?" A boy spoke on the other end. He sounded nervous.

Molly froze.

She recognized the voice.

"Matt?" she asked.

"Yeah, hi. I just called to say hello."

"Hello," Molly murmured, stunned.

"Your voice sounds different today," Matt observed. "Are you okay?"

Christina set down the milk container. "Who is it?" she asked Molly.

Molly dropped the phone, letting it thud against the

wall and then dangle on its cord. "What's wrong?" Ashley asked as Molly dashed into Christina's bathroom in the hall beside the kitchen. The sound of the door slamming shut was the only reply she received.

With a disturbed, puzzled expression, Christina lifted the bobbing phone. "Hello?"

"Christina, what's going on?"

"Who is this?" she asked, an uneasy feeling gripping her.

"Matt. I just told you that."

Christina felt her blood grow icy. "Uh-oh," she muttered.

"Christina, would it be better if I called back some other time?" Matt asked.

"Uh . . . um . . ." It was a harder question than he knew.

"Is something wrong?" he asked.

"Oh, yeah," she replied, her voice coming out in a shaking quiver. "You could definitely say that."

They hung on the phone, speechless. Christina watched as Ashley rapped on the bathroom door. Molly wouldn't answer her. "Matt, I think I'd better say good-bye. Well, good-bye."

"Bye," he said, sounding totally perplexed.

Hanging up, Christina stood a moment with her hand still on the phone, listening to the jackhammer beating of her heart. The worst had happened. She hadn't expected it to happen so soon, though.

Katie had joined Ashley at the bathroom door. She turned to Christina. "She won't even answer us. What's going on?"

"That was Matt on the phone," Christina filled them in.

"For Molly or for you?" Ashley asked cautiously.

Christina pointed to herself.

"Oh, boy!" Ashley and Katie spoke together in one gloomy voice.

Now what? Christina wondered as a pain formed in the pit of her stomach. What would she say to Molly now?

8

Molly gripped the sink in Christina's bathroom to steady herself until she finally stopped shaking and crying. This was so unbelievable. How could Christina do this to her? Christina, of all people, the person she'd thought was the kindest, truest friend she'd ever had. She felt so totally and completely betrayed, it made her head spin.

Sitting on the edge of the tub, Molly buried her face in her hands. The spinning stopped, but her stomach lurched. Fighting down the nausea, she clung to the shower curtain.

The wave of nausea finally ebbed. She turned on the faucet and splashed cool water on her face. She had to get away as quickly as possible. She needed some time to think.

Sucking in a deep, calming breath, Molly opened the door and walked out of Christina's bathroom with as much calm dignity as she could muster. She refused to let the girls see her cry.

Christina rushed to her. "Molly, you've got to believe me. I had no idea he was going to call. I don't even know why he did. Maybe it was something about Children's House." Her words tumbled from her in a frantic, panicked rush.

"Yeah, sure," Molly scoffed in a dry, bitter voice. She didn't want to hear it. She didn't believe it. Matt had admitted he liked another girl. And now Molly knew who it was.

At the kitchen phone, Molly called home and asked that someone come to pick her up. Her mother agreed to send the new chauffeur with the limo right away.

"Don't wait out there," Ashley begged Molly as she pulled on her jacket. "Stay in here and talk. We can sort this all out."

"No, sorry," Molly replied stiffly. "I'd rather be alone if you don't mind."

"Molly, please. This isn't my fault," Christina pleaded. "You've got to believe me."

"It really isn't," Ashley concurred, standing beside Christina.

Molly glared scornfully at both of them. Of course they'd stick together. They were so close. Katie just stood there, looking helpless. Molly could feel tears forming in the corners of her eyes.

"I thought you were my friend, and all the while you were trying to take away my boyfriend," Molly accused Christina coldly.

"I wasn't! I didn't!" Christina stammered.

"And if you knew how much she likes him, you'd see how hard that was for her!" Katie burst forth.

Christina gaped at Katie, horrified.

"Well, it's true," Katie insisted, tossing her hair back. "You're crazy about him but you held back. That's noble."

Too upset to say anything more without bursting into embarrassing tears, Molly spun away from them and slammed out through the door into the falling snow.

She ran down the drive as fast as the heavy snow would allow. White, fluffy drifts pulled at her boots as if they were trying to hold her back. Flakes got in her eyes, mixing with the salty, warm tears that blurred her vision. Roughly, she brushed them away.

By the time she reached the road, Molly could see tiny headlights glowing through the gray field of falling snow. To her great relief, she soon saw it was the limo coming to whisk her away.

She thought the new driver made a strange sight, his long overcoat flapping over his dark gray uniform, his head bent against the falling snow, as he rounded the front of the limo. He pulled open the back door for Molly, and she scrambled inside, grateful for the heat and the soft seats.

Brushing snowflakes from her clothes, Molly leaned forward and slid over the glass panel that separated her from the driver. "Thanks for coming out in this weather," she said.

"No problem, Miss," he replied in a voice rich with an Irish brogue.

"What's your name?"

"Seamus O'Legan, Miss," the driver replied as he tipped his hat.

"Don't call me 'Miss,' please," Molly said. "I'm Molly."

"Molly. A fine Irish name for a fine lass," Seamus said with approval.

"I'm named for my grandmother. She was Irish."

"It's a fine thing to be named for a relative," Seamus commented.

"Yes, I suppose so. I look like her, too."

Seamus nodded but said no more. Leaving the window between them open, Molly sank back into the cushiony leather seat and gazed out the window. The snow was falling so heavily now that she couldn't see much else.

When they returned to the house, Molly thanked Seamus again, then ran inside just long enough to grab her ice skates from the front hall closet.

"Molly, hi." Her mother, a delicate, meticulously groomed woman with a perfectly coiffed white-blonde bob, had come up quietly behind her. Molly turned, skates in hand. "Going skating?" she asked, eyeing the white leather skates.

"Just down to the pond," Molly replied hurriedly. She turned her face away so her mother wouldn't detect that she'd been crying.

"Are you all right, dear?" her mother asked, her brow furrowed with concern.

"Uh-huh," Molly lied. "The snow got in my eyes, but that's okay. It's so beautiful out. I haven't skated much at all this year, and I figured this would be a perfect day to start practicing again."

"Would you like to start taking figure skating lessons again?" her mother asked eagerly. "I think you're healthy enough now."

"Maybe," Molly agreed. She'd dropped the lessons when her anorexia had become really severe. The family therapist she and her parents had seen had suggested that anything that might put pressure or stress on Molly should be put on hold. The figure skating instruction she'd taken since she was four was one of the things she'd dropped, along with ballet lessons.

Really, though, right now she just wanted to get away from everyone.

Once she was back outside, Molly went through the formal garden and out onto the wide, gently sloping expanse of lawn, tromping through the ever-deepening snow. Off to the side of the lawn was a pond about the size of a tennis court. A huge elm tree spread over the pond. The graceful elm was lovely in spring, summer, and fall, its leaves making playful patterns on the sparkling water. But now its branches spread out like the fingers of an ominous skeleton.

That's all right, Molly thought, glancing up at the branches as she put her foot on a stone garden bench and laced her skate. She felt gloomy, dark, and skeletal right now. The tree looked just right.

The snow hadn't yet accumulated much on the pond. She would still be able to skate over the light dusting on top of the ice. Stepping out onto the frozen surface, Molly executed a graceful figure eight. Then she began speed-skating around the edges of the pond, going faster and faster until she had built up enough momentum to try a jump. A neat single axel.

Yes! She could still do it.

Molly smiled to herself as she skated backward,

regaining her breath. There were a lot of things she did well. The therapy sessions she'd been through had helped her to see that. She still sometimes felt that nothing she did was good enough for her parents, but she fought hard against that feeling. She knew they were proud of the way she had battled her illness, and she knew they would always love her. Not surrendering to that feeling of insecurity helped her to not give in to her anorexic tendencies.

It was stupid, anyway. Looking at herself from the outside, she knew people saw her as very pretty. She was talented, too. She could skate and dance, and she'd been captain of the cheerleading squad before she'd dropped out.

She'd been popular, too, at least with a certain crowd of kids before she'd decided to drop them. What a laugh. She'd thought they were shallow fakes. She'd believed her new friends were sincere, caring, and loyal, by far superior to her old friends in every way. Ha! They were just the same, worse even.

Molly spun in a neat circle. Okay, so maybe it wasn't fair to blame Katie and Ashley for this mess. But they'd stuck up for Christina. Besides, Christina had been the one she was really close to—or *thought* she was close to.

In a way, she couldn't totally blame Matt for feeling as he did. She'd changed dramatically in the last few months. After all, he'd started going steady with the old Molly, not with the person she'd become. How could she expect him to still like her when she'd become so different?

Her spinning slowed, and she began skating fluidly around the pond. Up until this minute, she'd assumed the "new" Molly was an improvement over the old. But maybe she wasn't. Matt obviously didn't think so.

Molly kicked her leg out to the side and went into another rapid turn. When she was done, she felt elated and breathless.

She'd also come to a decision. If Matt liked the old Molly, she'd go back to being that person. This experience with change had been a bomb. The friends she'd thought she could count on had let her down. From now on, she didn't need anyone.

Except Matt—and she was determined to get him back.

An idea made Molly snap her fingers with excitement. What better way to signal to the world that the old Molly was back than to win the title of Most Popular for the school yearbook?

She could, too, if she set her mind to it. Molly knew it would take work. Before she was hospitalized, she had been very popular. She'd hung out with the right people and had been involved in lots of activities. She'd been out of circulation for the last few months, and she'd lost a lot of ground. But she could make it up.

She had to. And she would, no matter what it took.

On her way back to the house, Molly saw her father moving across the snowy yard with Liam on his arm. The sun had begun to set, and it threw a pink glow over the house and grounds. She realized they were heading for the old stone triple-car garage that her father had set up as a painting studio.

Cutting across the snow-covered lawn, Molly ran toward the building, arriving just as they neared its front door. "Hi, Molly," her father greeted her. "Liam woke from his nap, so I decided to bring him to my studio. I thought I might do a bit of work before dinner."

"Can I come along?" Molly asked breathlessly.

"Of course." Her father smiled and turned the key in the door.

The three entered the empty building. Mr. Morgan had moved a refrigerator, a table, and a couch into the low-ceilinged first floor. With Mr. Morgan carefully guiding Liam, they went up the narrow stairs and walked into the studio loft.

Like the downstairs, the second story also had a low ceiling. Pink light from the snow-filled sky poured into the room through a large picture window. A paint-spattered easel, a table, and an overstuffed chair beside the window were the only furniture. Mr. Morgan gently eased Liam into the chair. Then he opened the closet door and took out a blank canvas. "Might as well begin a new painting," he explained. "Something wonderful may happen."

Mr. Morgan set the canvas on the easel. His paints were neatly laid out on the table beside it. "Can I see what you worked on while you were in Ireland?" Molly requested.

"Sorry," her father replied, studying the blank canvas thoughtfully. "I didn't want to carry the paintings, so I had them shipped. Hopefully they'll arrive tomorrow or the next day."

He lifted a piece of charcoal from his table and began

to quickly outline an image. "I'm starting a series on the castle," he explained.

"Aren't you going to work from a sketch?" Molly asked.

"Not this time. I made a million sketches in Ireland, but I want to capture my impression of the castle, not its exact details. I'm only laying in the barest outlines, then I'll begin to paint from memory."

As he worked, sketching in bold strokes, Molly glanced at Liam. If he'd been interested in the process of her father's work back in Ireland, he wasn't now. He gazed out the window at the stark trees waving in the pink sky.

Yet, Molly noticed something. His expression wasn't entirely blank. His brow had creased. He seemed almost to frown.

Curious, Molly went to the window to see what he was looking at.

A flock of Canadian geese was crossing the snowy sky in a *V*, their bodies black silhouettes, their wings gracefully carrying them through the fat white flakes that fell silently to the ground.

Looking back at Liam, Molly started. The boy's eyes were wet with tears. As salty tear tracks ran down his alabaster skin, Liam's entire attention remained locked on the geese.

Mr. Morgan was completely engrossed in his sketch and didn't notice what was happening. Molly didn't say anything to him. Somehow this moment seemed so private. She had the strangest feeling that to speak about it, to point Liam's tears out to her father, would be some sort of betrayal.

So, instead, she simply turned toward the window and watched with Liam until the *V* formation of soaring geese disappeared from the darkening sky.

9

That night Ashley and Katie slept at Christina's, snuggled in sleeping bags in front of the fire blazing in the fireplace.

Ashley insisted Christina take the soft brown couch. "You've had a rotten afternoon, and you need a good night's sleep. If I get too uncomfortable down here, I'll go into your bed," Ashley said. She felt so sorry for Christina, she wanted to do everything possible to be kind to her.

Despite the snow, Ashley could have easily made it home. Her house was just up the drive, less than a three-minute walk. But Christina was so distraught about what had happened with Molly that Ashley wanted to stay to comfort her friend.

When Katie called home to ask if she could stay, Aunt Rainie was more than happy to agree. "I'm glad we don't have to come get you in this storm," she said. "The driving conditions are terrible. It took me an hour just to get home from work. I couldn't see a thing in front of me. Have a nice time, Katie, hon."

The girls talked until one in the morning. They talked about the angels and their latest encounter on the bridge. But mostly they talked about Matt and Molly, discussing how unfair it was for Molly to be angry when Christina had never done anything dishonest. After a while, their eyes grew heavy and they settled down to sleep.

In the middle of the night, though, Ashley's eyes drifted open. At first, she wasn't sure where she was. She blinked hard, then remembered when she turned and looked into the fireplace.

The fire had dissolved into glowing embers. They crackled softly, dancing over the charred ashes every now and then. In the dying orange light, everything in the living room took on a soft, golden glow. Ashley pushed up onto her elbows and blew a red curl from her sleepy eyes.

Outside, the wind howled like a crazy animal. It battered against the window, as if trying to break in. Swirls of white snow climbed up onto the frosty windowpanes. Every few minutes Ashley heard something bang, kicked over by the wild, screaming wind.

It made her grateful to be inside. She felt like a small animal in a cozy, warm den—a mouse, maybe, buried deep under the ground. She wondered about other, unsheltered animals, like the deer or the birds. Where were they now? Silently, she sent up a quick prayer for them. Did angels watch over animals, too? Somehow she knew Ned, Norma, and Edwina would.

With these thoughts in her head, she fell back to sleep, but she had an unsettling dream. She was walking into the stable and realized something was very wrong. It was too quiet. There was an unfamiliar smell in the air. Then it hit her. All the horses were gone! Every single one of them!

"No!" Ashley cried in her dream. "Junior! Daisy! Bridey! Clover!" She called their names as she tore through the stable, searching for any sign of them. Maybe they were all out on a trail ride. She hurried outside. No one was around. As she ran into the woods, she tripped over something. Looking down, she saw four small toy sailboats, each with a single sail. Scooping them up, she began to weep as if her heart were breaking.

Ashley awakened in the dark room and discovered that her eyes were wet with tears. "Four sailboats?" she murmured. How strange? Why had the sailboats made her so sad?

The answer came to her in a flash of insight. Four sails. For sale. It was a dream about the ranch being for sale.

No. No. No. Her mind rejected this idea completely. They weren't in that much trouble, were they? She didn't think so. But even the idea of losing the ranch was upsetting. She'd always lived here. It had been in her family for years.

Unable to fall back to sleep, Ashley wriggled out of her sleeping bag. Katie snored softly beside her, strands of her rich auburn hair falling across her peaceful face. Christina was curled up in a ball on the couch.

The fire was out now, and the room had grown chilly. Ashley stood and realized something had changed. The howling wind had died down. Glancing at the window, she saw that the endless flakes of snow had stopped falling.

Ashley yanked the plaid throw blanket from the arm of a chair. She wrapped the warm wool fabric around her shoulders like a shawl as she walked to the window and peered out. "Ah," she sighed, the sound escaping her lips without her even realizing.

Outside, a full moon shone brilliantly in the clear sky, lighting the unmarked snowdrifts. She guessed it must be knee-deep at least, higher where the drifts had accumulated. In the moonlight the snow sparkled as if the stars in the sky had somehow been pulled to earth and captured within the perfect crystals of snow.

With her face close to the window, Ashley continued to gaze out, marveling at the amazing beauty. She longed to be outside, to be part of it.

But that was crazy. It was freezing.

Suddenly swept with quiet excitement, Ashley went to the chair where she'd neatly folded her clothes. Pulling on her jeans, she swiftly tucked in the flannel nightshirt she'd borrowed from Christina. Then she bundled herself into her jacket, gloves, and boots. In minutes, she was dressed and ready to go.

Quietly pulling open the door, Ashley stepped out into the silent, moonlit night. The wind wasn't completely gone. The towering, snow-laden pines across the drive danced in the breeze, their pine needles rubbing. In the distance she could hear the wind whispering among the branches, although it no longer raged. Now it sang a sort of calling song, like mermaids on a cliff luring passing sailors.

The moon's light soaked everything so that it was easy for Ashley to see where she was going. And, strangely, the air didn't feel very cold.

Moved by something within her heart, Ashley started to walk away from the house. Her boots made a crackling sound as she broke through the crust of ice that had formed on top of the snow. Ashley realized it was this icy layer that made everything shine so.

How wonderful to be out on this magic night. Ashley imagined she was the only living creature awake on the earth at that moment, the only one drinking in this awesome sight.

She continued making her way toward the road. When she was almost there, she stopped abruptly. She gasped, eyes wide, her gloved hands flying to her cheeks.

Out in the pasture, in the spot where the girls had built the snow angel, stood a giant, shimmering angel! She was almost ten feet high, and her wings spread majestically, inviting Ashley to come closer. Varying shades of blue, yellow, pink, and purple surrounded her, creating a dazzling mosaic of sparkling, other-worldly light.

This was certainly not the angel they'd built. This was some sort of miracle.

Slowly, Ashley approached the glistening figure, ducking between the fence rails and making a trail of deep footsteps through the snow-filled pasture. As she drew closer, Ashley could see the luminous angel in greater detail.

Her face was delicate and beautiful. She seemed to smile down gently at Ashley. Long, flowing waves of snowy hair curled around her graceful neck and shoulders.

Gazing up at her, Ashley suddenly realized why the angel had been sent. It was an answer to the request she'd made that day on the bridge.

The snow angel had been sent by Ned, Norma, and Edwina to help Ashley save the ranch.

10

On Sunday morning, Molly couldn't resist peeking into the guest room where Liam slept. She'd found the door slightly ajar, and she assumed her father had left it open so he would be able to hear Liam if he cried out during the night.

The frail boy lay under the covers, his head turned toward her, dark curls splashed across the crisp white pillowcase. With his face at rest and those unsettling, staring eyes closed, Molly thought he looked very handsome.

With silent steps, she stole into the room, curious. Liam's suitcase lay open on the floor beside his bed. Molly noticed a hardcover maroon book, half covered by a pair of jeans. Kneeling, she lifted the slim volume from the suitcase. The word "Journal" was embossed in neat gold script on the front cover.

Molly jiggled the book in her hands. The temptation to open it was irresistible, although she knew she shouldn't invade Liam's privacy. *I'll just read the last few pages*, she promised herself. Molly reasoned that reading about Liam might help her understand him. If she understood, maybe she could even help him while he was here.

With a quivering hand, she quickly opened the journal and flipped through to the spot where the writing ended.

> *Going riding with Brian tomorrow morning. I hope that horse of his behaves. I admire Fiona's high spirits, but she gets spooked so easily. We've decided to ride up above the cliffs since the weather will be good. I love it up there, wild and beautiful. To-night Dad and I watched a semifinal football match on television. Dad nearly jumped out of his chair when his team lost! Mum cooked a stew with brussels sprouts in it. I nearly gagged!*

Molly smiled. Liam sounded so sweet, like someone she could easily be friends with. Or could have been before the accident.

"Spying on our guest?"

Molly startled and whirled around to see her father standing in the doorway wearing his heavy green plaid robe and slippers. His dark, graying hair was still tousled from sleep. She hadn't even heard him! "Wow! You scared me!" she scolded in a whisper.

He nodded down at the book in her hands and scowled reprovingly.

Molly looked guiltily at her father. She slapped Liam's journal shut and placed it back in the suitcase, tucking it under the jeans just as she'd found it. "I thought Liam's journal might tell me something about him so I could help him," she explained quietly.

Mr. Morgan put his arm around Molly's shoulders and steered her back out into the hall. "Conor packed it in the hope that Liam might start writing again even if he wouldn't speak."

"He hasn't," Molly reported. "The last time he wrote was before the accident. He sounded so happy, Dad. It's hard to believe the boy you brought home is the same boy who wrote those words."

Mrs. Morgan came down the hall toward them. Molly marveled at how her mother always looked so well-groomed, even in the early hours of the morning. Her blunt blonde bob was combed, her royal blue robe fresh. She even wore a dab of pink lipstick. She smiled sleepily at them. "What are you two doing up so early on a Sunday morning?"

"I woke up a while ago and couldn't get back to sleep," Molly told her.

"Something on your mind?" Mrs. Morgan asked. "Do you want to talk about it?"

"No," Molly replied, almost too quickly. In truth, she had been up thinking about Matt since dawn. But she didn't feel like discussing her boyfriend problems with her parents. They'd probably just tell her she'd meet lots of other boys and that she was a pretty girl and she shouldn't worry about Matt. She wasn't in the mood to hear this.

"Why are you up so early?" Mrs. Morgan turned the question on her husband.

"Jet lag, I think," he replied, gently shutting Liam's door all the way. "After all that time in Ireland and the time change coming home, my internal clock is all confused."

"I hate that feeling," Mrs. Morgan sympathized. "Actually, I woke early and couldn't go back to sleep, either. The Daughters of Heritage board of directors put me in charge of finding a local charity to support for our winter benefit, and I just haven't any idea where to begin looking."

"There's that new soup kitchen and food pantry in town," Mr. Morgan offered.

Mrs. Morgan's eyes lit enthusiastically. "Yes! What's it called? Come and Get It? Come Quick?"

"Come On Inn," Mr. Morgan told her.

"That's right!" Mrs. Morgan said. "Cute name. It might be perfect."

"The time change must have affected my stomach, too," Mr. Morgan complained. "I'm hungry. Anyone feel like going out for breakfast?"

"No thanks," Mrs. Morgan declined. "I want to call Harriet Hanson right away and see what she thinks of this idea. We'll have to form a committee to study it, of course. We wouldn't want to back a disreputable charity." With a distracted wave, Molly's mother turned and disappeared down the hall, obviously absorbed in this new project.

Mr. Morgan turned to Molly. "How about breakfast and a good long chat, Molly? Just the two of us."

"Sure," Molly agreed enthusiastically. Sunday was Joy's day off, and meals were usually leftovers since neither of Molly's parents enjoyed cooking. Besides, Molly was eager to spend some time alone with her father. She'd really missed seeing him the past few weeks.

"Do you think the roads are clear enough to drive on?" she questioned.

Mr. Morgan frowned thoughtfully. "Today's Seamus's day off." He checked the gleaming mahogany clock on a side table in the hall. "Mr. O'Legan's a pleasant fellow, don't you think?"

"I haven't spoken to him much, but he seems very nice."

"He drove for me while I was in Ireland. It was quite remarkable, really. A few days before I was due to come home, he arrived on the doorstep. He told me he had been promised a job on a cruise ship, but it wasn't due to start for about a month. He wanted to know if I perhaps needed a driver for a few weeks. I knew Franklin wanted some time off, so I checked Seamus's references and invited him to come over with us and fill in. I liked him immediately."

Molly nodded. "So you're saying you'll have to do the driving today. I bet the plows have cleared the roads by now."

"You're probably right," Mr. Morgan agreed. "We'll take your mother's car. It handles well in the snow, and I can't imagine she'd want to go out in this weather."

"I'll be dressed in a sec," Molly told him. Running to her room, she wriggled out of her nightshirt and threw on her clothes. She slipped her woolen socks on and decided to let her blonde hair hang loose to save time.

In the hall closet she found her lace-up snow boots and warm wool-lined parka. She put her cellular phone in its bag over her shoulder and then zipped her jacket shut over it.

Molly was ready to go by the time her father met her at the front door. "I called the country club. They're serving breakfast this morning despite the snow." He hesitated. "Oh, dear, I forgot. You hate the Pine Ridge Country Club, don't you?"

Molly wrinkled her nose. "I don't hate it, Dad. It's just that some of the people there are so snobby."

"True," he agreed. "It's a great club, however, and they have a wonderful brunch." He snapped his fingers. "Doesn't the Pine Manor Inn serve brunch on Sundays? Would you rather go there?"

Molly looked disdainfully at her father. "I don't want to go to that dump."

Mr. Morgan's eyes widened in surprise. "Dump? I was under the impression that the Pine Manor Ranch rated extremely high in your esteem."

"It used to," Molly said curtly.

"What happened?" he asked with barely concealed dismay.

"Nothing very important." She brushed off the query with a wave of her hand. "Besides, the inn closes for the winter." As she spoke, she remembered her decision to return to her former ways. Maybe she'd see some of her old friends at the club. She could rebuild some of her relationships with kids who were popular and whose parents had money. Kids more like herself than Ashley, Katie, and Christina. "The club is fine," she said. "Let's go."

When they pulled out onto the road in her mother's dark green car, they found that it had indeed been plowed. Navigating the winding roads was easy. The problem came when they turned onto the narrow road that passed by the Pine Manor Ranch.

"Dad, look out!" Molly cried, realizing that the car in front of them wasn't moving.

Mr. Morgan jammed on the brakes. The car swerved, first to the right, then to the left. "The road's too icy!" he cried. "I've lost control!"

Molly sat up straight in her seat and closed her eyes.

With a jarring thud, she felt the car bounce over something, then shudder to a stop. When she opened her eyes, Molly saw that the car was perched on a steep angle. Her right side was pressed against the passenger-side door.

"Are you all right, Molly?" her father asked shakily as he struggled to sit up straight.

"Yes. You?"

"Fine," Mr. Morgan said, regaining his composure. "But we seem to be in rather a bad spot."

Looking around, she saw that they'd careened into a snowdrift off to the side of the road. The car had landed against something under the snow and was tilted upward, its right side lower than its left.

With great effort, Mr. Morgan pushed open his door

and jumped out. Reaching back in and extending his hand to Molly, he pulled her out the driver's side door after him. They looked ahead and saw that they were at the tail end of a long line of stopped cars, a traffic jam. Molly guessed that everyone in Pine Ridge must be on this road today.

The clip-clop of hooves made Molly turn. A police officer mounted on a large black horse had come upon them. He was dressed in a heavy jacket and a police hat with the earflaps down. He wore dark sunglasses to shield his eyes from the blinding glare of sunlight on snow. "You folks all right?" he inquired from atop his horse.

"Fine, except for the car," Mr. Morgan replied. "I think I'll need a tow truck. What's going on? Has there been an accident?"

"Everyone's come out to see some kind of miracle or something up at the ranch," the police officer told him. "Some kind of a snow angel."

Molly's mind reeled. A snow angel? Surely it couldn't be the angel they'd built yesterday. It was nice, but . . . a miracle? Not quite.

The officer chuckled. "Yeah, two snowplow drivers noticed it around dawn this morning. They started talking about it down at Jimmy's Diner, and news spread fast. You know how it goes around these parts. Talk, talk, talk."

Molly peered up at the policeman. She couldn't see his name tag, but she wondered if it said "Officer Winger." Since becoming aware of the angels, she, Ashley, Christina, and Katie had also become aware of the many, very different-looking Officer Wingers in their area. Ned, Norma, and Edwina had told the girls that these special angels were everywhere. Something about the way this officer had appeared so suddenly made Molly absolutely sure he was one of them.

"I can call a tow truck to come out here for you," the officer offered.

"Great." Mr. Morgan accepted. "I have a card with my name and address right here." He took his wallet from his inside coat pocket and opened it, but the police officer waved his hand. "No need. I know who you are, Mr. Morgan."

Her father's eyes flashed with astonishment. "You do? How?"

"Like I said, everybody talks around here. It's a small town."

"Yes, I suppose so," Mr. Morgan said, looking unconvinced. "Could you have them take the car back to my house?"

"No problem. Why don't you head up and see the angel while I take care of this for you," the officer suggested.

Molly's father looked at her. "We might as well see what all the fuss is about," he agreed. "Do you want to walk up?"

"Yes." The fact was she couldn't get there fast enough. She was dying to know what was going on.

"How on earth is he going to call for help on his horse?" Mr. Morgan muttered as they started walking up the road past the idling cars.

Molly recalled the cellular phone in the bag slung over

her shoulder. She turned back to the policeman. "I have a phone. Do you want to use it to call the tow company?" she offered.

"No thanks." The officer declined with a smile. "I'm fine."

With a shrug, Molly turned back to her father, and they continued walking. The cars coughed exhaust clouds of dirty white smoke out of their tailpipes and into the crisp, cold air. The snow along the side of the road was already blackened.

Opening her jacket, Molly took her phone out of its pouch and quickly punched in Ashley's number. "Maybe I can find out what's going on," she told her father.

No one answered at Ashley's, however. Molly hung up on the phone machine without leaving a message. Normally she would have tried Christina next, but there was no way she was about to call *her* today, or anytime soon. If Molly wasn't desperate with curiosity, she would have just sat in the car and waited for the tow truck to come. When she awoke this morning, the ranch was the last place she'd have pictured herself today.

As they neared the entrance to the ranch, Molly and her father saw that all the cars were headed into it. "This must be quite a sight," Mr. Morgan commented.

"Yeah," Molly murmured.

Mr. Morgan stopped. "I just thought of something," he said, frowning. "Mom can't come get us because she doesn't know how to drive the other cars. They're all standard shift, and she only drives automatic. I'll phone the club. Someone there can pick us up. Let's see, who's always at brunch on Sunday? I usually see Robert Tellers there . . ."

As he spoke, Molly glanced back at the car.

"Dad, look!" she cried, clutching his arm.

Mr. Morgan turned to see what Molly was so excited about. He gasped at what he saw.

The car was completely righted. It stood on the side of the road as if nothing had ever happened. And the officer on horseback was gone.

Mr. Morgan looked at Molly, his eyes wide. "Now how do you suppose he managed that?"

Molly spoke with assurance. "I think he might have been an angel, Dad."

Mr. Morgan's eyes went even wider, though he didn't scoff. "An angel," he said pensively. "A police angel on horseback? I suppose it's possible. Quite unlikely, but possible. Do you really think so?"

Molly nodded.

She knew he was open to the idea. They'd talked about angels after her father had been saved by one in Ireland when they were there together. In fact, it was that encounter with an angel that had changed Mr. Morgan. He had been distant and wrapped up in his work before. But the angel had made Mr. Morgan realize that his family was important, and he had decided to quit his job and spend more time with them. He and Molly had never been closer, and Molly had never been happier.

They stared at their car for several minutes more as, behind them, the long line of cars continued to crawl into the ranch. Finally, Mr. Morgan looked at Molly brightly, as if throwing off the mantle of awe that had enveloped them in its spell. "Well, speaking of angels, let's go see this so-called snow angel."

11

Christina was barely aware of the continual seemingly endless line of cars pouring into the driveway or of the murmuring crowd forming around the snow angel. She stood transfixed, mouth agape, eyes wide, as if the only two beings on earth were herself and this strange, gorgeous creature.

She stared long and hard at the ice-covered angel, drinking in every detail. The pine cone hair was now lost, buried somewhere inside. In its place were icicle curls of swirling frozen water. The wind had drifted the snow on the face into a gently smiling countenance. The angel's eyes were only half open, and it made her seem to be looking down on everyone who stood around her. Her form, robes, hands, even the delicate feet that showed at the hem of her gown, had been sculpted in snow by the wind, and then coated completely in a crust of shining ice.

"Unbelievable, isn't she?" said Ashley, who'd come up silently beside Christina. Katie stood next to Ashley, and both girls gazed up reverently at the angel.

"Beyond unbelievable." Christina murmured an awe-filled reply.

"It's amazing to think that nature did this," Katie commented.

"What?" Christina stared at her in disbelief.

"Well, what do *you* think made it?" Katie shot back.

"Angels, of course," Christina declared certainly. How could Katie think that this perfect creation was the work of nature alone?

"Oh, come on," Katie scoffed. "The snow piled up on the original form, and then the wind swirled it around, and the whole thing iced over. I mean, it's beautiful and all, but so are icicles and snowdrifts and the pines with snow on them."

"How can you compare those to this?" Christina cried, aghast at the idea. "Look at the face."

"I know. It looks really real. But so does the face of the man in the moon," Katie argued.

Ashley cut in. "Nature does some miraculous things," she said. "In this case, though, I agree with Christina. This angel is more than an accident of nature."

Katie scowled. "I don't know."

Christina knew, though. *Thank you for answering me*, she said silently. Certainly this angel was her answer. It was a sign that she was on the right track with her beliefs. There were forces in the world— unexplainable, mystical forces—that couldn't be seen but were nonetheless real.

"It looks like someone dragged something to the angel," Katie noted.

Christina followed the direction of Katie's glance. There was a track through the snow leading from the fence to the angel. She gasped. "Do you think the angel moved? By itself?"

"No," Ashley said quickly. "It was me. Last night I got the painting ladder from the supply shed. I wanted to get a closer look at the angel's face."

"You dragged a ladder all the way through the snow in the middle of the night?" Katie questioned.

Ashley shrugged self-consciously and said, "It seemed important at the time."

"Sure it was important." Christina backed Ashley up. "There she was in the middle of the night looking at a miracle in the middle of the pasture. Of course she wanted a closer look."

"Okay, if you say so," Katie said doubtfully.

Christina glanced over her shoulder. The crowd behind them was growing, and she recognized a lot of the people from town: old Mr. and Mrs. O'Herlihy from the food market; Mr. Fisher, the lawyer, and Mrs. Fisher, a teacher at school; Amy Thomasan, who ran Amy's Academy of Dance over the post office. Glancing at the cars, she noticed the red Jeep driven by Dr. Jeffers, the local veterinarian. The crowd also contained faces that weren't familiar. She was amazed that the news had spread so quickly.

On the other side of the angel, Alice stood next to Ashley's mother and father. Jeremy and Jason, Ashley's twin brothers, stood a little ways off with a cluster of their high school friends. Champ leaped through the snow excitedly.

"It seems like the whole world is here," Ashley noted happily.

"I'll say," Katie agreed. She pointed suddenly at the line of cars. "Look!"

A shining blue truck was coming up the drive. The letters WPNE, the call letters from the local television station, were stenciled in white on the side. "Okay!" Ashley cheered softly. "This is just what I've been waiting for."

"What do you mean?" Christina asked.

Ashley looked away, as if embarrassed or distressed.

"Waiting for what?" Christina pressed.

Ashley turned back to her. "I just mean that . . . well . . . that I'm glad the angel is bringing so much attention to the ranch. It . . . it's what I asked for on the bridge."

"You did?" Christina cried. "So, in a way, this angel answered you and me, both." She explained what she'd asked for. "Maybe it's here for all of us. What did you ask for, Katie?"

Katie pressed her lips together, as though she didn't want to answer.

"Maybe it's too personal," Ashley said quickly.

"No, no, I'll tell you," Katie relented. "I thought it sounded sort of weird, but I'll tell you. You're my best friends, after all. I've been feeling kind of depressed about the way people act toward each other. I asked for some sort of sign that people aren't all bad. People seem like such creeps sometimes, but I don't want to think everyone is like that."

"Is that what you think?" Christina asked.

"Sometimes. A lot of the time," she admitted.

"But what about us, and your aunt and uncle?" Ashley asked.

"Of course none of you are that way. But I listen to the news, and I read about all the mean, cruel things people do. It gets me down."

Christina gazed up at the angel. If this angel was answering Katie, she didn't see how. "Maybe something will happen to change your mind," she said softly.

"What do you mean?" Katie asked.

"Maybe because of this angel you'll be able to see the good in people."

Behind them car horns began to blare. The TV truck had stopped. Two men climbed out and began unloading equipment, blocking everyone else who was trying to get past. In the car directly behind the truck, a man stuck his head out the window. "Move that truck!" he screamed before hurling a curse at the driver.

In the car behind him, another man stuck his head out his open window. "Watch your fat mouth, you slob. I got kids in this car!" he bellowed. The three blond boys in the backseat pressed their faces against the inside of the window, making them appear monstrously flattened.

Katie chuckled bitterly. "Oh, you mean like right now?" she asked Christina ironically. "This is a nice display of human loveliness."

"No, not exactly right now, I guess," Christina conceded.

Ignoring the horns and the shouting man, the news crew—two cameramen and a woman reporter—trudged through the snow, the men hoisting large cameras on their shoulders, the woman holding a silvery microphone.

"Wow! It looks like we're going to be on the news," Katie said.

"Yes!" Ashley said, making a small, excited pumping motion with her balled fists.

Shifting her eyes back to the angel, Christina wondered aloud, "What could Molly have asked for? I wonder if this angel somehow has an answer for her, too?"

"Speaking of Molly," Katie said.

Christina looked up and saw Molly and her father slipping under the opening in the split rail fence. She hadn't expected to see Molly. Certainly not today.

She was glad to see her, though. If Molly had come to the ranch, maybe she wanted to talk. Perhaps this wasn't the end of their friendship, after all.

Heartened, Christina waved to Molly. But Molly either didn't see her or pretended not to. Rising on her toes, Christina waved even harder. "Over here, Molly! We're over here."

Right then, a loud gasp of surprise swept through the crowd.

Looking back sharply, Christina checked the angel. She saw nothing new. "What happened?" she asked Ashley and Katie.

Both girls stood with their eyes riveted on the angel's face. Christina shook Katie's shoulder. "What happened?"

"The eyes," Katie murmured, not shifting her gaze from the angel's face. "Check out her eyes."

Christina looked up and peered into the angel's eyes,

but she didn't see anything strange. "I don't get it. What do—"

Christina stopped speaking. She'd seen the pulsating flashes of bright white light emanating from deep within the angel's icy, yet translucent eyes.

"We're blessed!" cried white-haired Mrs. O'Herlihy, dropping to her knees in the snow.

"Look! There it is again!" yelled one of Jason and Jeremy's friends, a girl with straight black hair.

Once again Christina saw the eyes pulse with flashing light.

Suddenly the reporter and her camera crew pushed their way through the crowd. The reporter stood beside the snow angel and waited for her cameramen to set their equipment up. Within minutes one of the cameramen signaled to her.

"This is Tammy Jacobs live at the Pine Manor Ranch." The reporter spoke in the crisp, studied, upbeat voice of a trained announcer. "It's a miracle in the snow," she continued dramatically, her legs planted firmly, her chin lifted. "Last night the howling winds swept an awe-inspiring, heavenly visitor into the sleepy, rural town of Pine Ridge. This intriguing snow sculpture has already profoundly affected the massive crowd that has turned out to see it this freezing winter morning. I'm told this huge figure sits upon the base of a much smaller angel that was built yesterday by four local girls. Just now people here witnessed what many are already calling a miracle—an unearthly light flashing from the angel's eyes. Is it just a trick of sunlight on ice, or is it indeed a spiritual message?"

A short woman, bundled in a woolen cap and so many heavy sweaters that only her glasses showed, hurried to Tammy Jacobs with a piece of paper. She pointed at Christina, Katie, and Ashley.

The announcer smiled enthusiastically into the camera. "I've just been informed that the girls who built the original angel are right here. Let's have a word with them."

12

Katie coughed nervously, her throat suddenly very dry. She was grasping for words to describe exactly what she wanted to say. Although she thought this angel might be some kind of special sign from Ned, Norma, and Edwina, Katie was still practical enough to know that it might be nothing more than the result of yesterday's snowstorm. She didn't want to sound like a flake on television.

Finally sure of her words, Katie lifted her gaze to the camera and began to speak.

"I don't really know how this beautiful angel got here, but I'm sure there's a logical explanation. I mean, the wind whips up some pretty awesome stuff when it's blowing snow around, and it was really windy last night. I saw the light in her eyes, but I think it was probably just the reflection of the sun on her face or something like that. I don't think people should get all freaked out about this. The angel is beautiful, but she's just a bunch of snow."

"What about you, young lady?" Tammy Jacobs turned to Ashley. Ashley beamed into the camera and began speaking right away.

"Spring is only several months away, and the Pine Manor Ranch offers the best in trail riding and horseback riding lessons, and it's an excellent place to board your horse. The Pine Manor Inn is right here, too. It's a great vacation spot the entire family can enjoy."

"But what do you think of this angel?" Tammy prompted.

"Oh—uh," Ashley stammered, glancing up quickly at the angel. "Everyone should come out to see her. She's awesome. And while you're here, don't forget to book your spring weekend getaway at the Pine Manor Inn."

"Thank you," Tammy said, turning her attention to Christina. "And how about you?"

Christina's eyes darted over to Molly, who had come to the front of the crowd. She hated seeing Molly on the outside, separate from them. "Molly helped build the snow angel, too." She pointed at her friend, wanting to bring her closer and to do something to heal the rift between them caused by the phone call from Matt.

She knew Molly blamed her for the breakup. Looking back over yesterday's events, Christina could even understand how Molly had jumped to the conclusion that she had tried to steal Matt, although that wasn't true. But Christina didn't care about any of that now. She only wanted to be friends again. She hoped Molly felt the same.

"Well, Molly," Tammy said, stepping toward her. "What do you think of this angel?"

Molly nervously pulled at the ends of her long blonde hair. "Well . . . I don't know, really. I personally believe in angels, so I think this beautiful snow statue must have been sent by angels. She must be here for a special reason."

"That's the truth!" shouted a woman standing behind Molly.

"I guess we'll never know for sure, though," Molly added hurriedly, somehow unnerved by the zealous fervor of the woman who had cried out. "Angels work in ways we don't always understand, so . . . so I guess we'll never know."

"Is that what you think?" Tammy turned the microphone to Christina.

"Yes, absolutely!" Christina concurred, smiling at Molly, glad to be in agreement. "Only more so. I know in my heart this angel is a miracle. I think she was sent here as a symbol of the real power that angels have in our lives. I think this angel is here to give people hope."

"So you believe in angels, too?" Tammy questioned.

Christina hesitated. She and her friends had long ago agreed not to tell other people about the angels. Ned, Norma, and Edwina were their own special angels, and they didn't want others to find out about them. The girls had even kept the angels a secret from their families. And they didn't want the peaceful Pine Manor woods trampled with curious people looking for angels at the Angel's Crossing Bridge.

Christina thought a moment longer. She decided she could say what she thought without revealing where the angels could be found.

"I've seen angels," she said solemnly. "With my own eyes. I know they're real."

13

Katie rested her head on her desk and watched the fat flakes of snow come down. The snow had begun again this morning while she waited for the school bus, and nearly another inch had already fallen.

She wondered what this new snow was doing to the snow angel. Would it cover her over? Would she grow even larger? Would the bitter cold deter the steady stream of people who came to the ranch to see her?

"Katie Nelson?" Mr. Palmero, her homeroom teacher called the roll.

"Here," she answered absently.

"Hey, Nelson," a boy across the aisle from her hissed. She looked over and faced Darrin Tyson, a burly boy with short blond hair and blue eyes. Darrin had delighted in bugging Katie ever since she came to Pine Ridge Middle School. He wasn't really a terrible guy, though, just a pest. "I saw you on the news," he said, grinning.

"Yeah, so?" Katie replied defensively, bracing for the insult. Darrin usually had one ready and waiting for her.

"You were the only one who didn't sound like a total lunatic," was his unexpected comment.

Katie frowned. Was Darrin actually paying her a compliment? Or would there be a punchline? "Thanks, I think," she said skeptically as she turned around in her seat.

Last night Katie and her whole family had crowded around the TV set to watch the evening news. Plump, frizzy-haired, good-hearted Aunt Rainie had been beside herself with excitement as she waited for the story about the snow angel. "Our Katie on TV! Imagine!"

Taciturn Uncle Jeff peered at the screen, frowning. "I don't trust those TV people," he muttered. Even sloppy, dark-haired Mel, who was normally so disinterested in her, watched the show with keen attention.

Seeing herself on TV was strange. So was seeing her friends. It was as though they were no longer real people, but characters on a show. "I look so tall," she commented.

"It's good to be tall," Aunt Rainie assured her. "You remind me of your mother more every day." Katie smiled at the comparison. Since her parents' tragic death in a car accident last year, she had been living with Aunt Rainie and Uncle Jeff. Sometimes she worried that she would forget about her parents, but moments like this made her feel that they would always be close to her.

When she'd arrived in school this morning, a lot of

kids said they'd seen the news. And everyone seemed to know about the angel. Everyone!

"How does it feel to be famous?" Darrin asked.

"I'm not famous," Katie said gruffly.

Darrin whistled softly and shook his head. "Yes, you are. Everyone around here is talking about that angel, and you helped build it."

"That angel is not the one we built," Katie corrected.

"I know" Darrin replied. "But you're involved with the biggest news in Pine Ridge in years. My mother took the morning off from work today so she could go see the angel."

"She *should* see it," Katie told him. "It's really beautiful."

"That's not why she's going. She's going to ask the angel for something. I think she's asking for my aunt, her sister, to have a baby because she hasn't been able to or something."

Katie shrugged. She didn't know what to think about that. She didn't know what to think about any of this. It totally confused her. The truth was, although she wanted to believe the angel was just a creation of wind and snow, she wasn't so sure.

After all, the girls had been to the bridge, and they'd each asked for things. Although Ashley and Christina were sure the snow angel was the answer to their requests, Katie didn't see how the angel fit in with what she'd asked for. She didn't feel any better about people as a result of seeing it. In fact, many of the people who had poured in to see the angel had been rude to one another. Some had fought over parking and pushed each other in their efforts to get closer. The angel certainly hadn't brought out the best in the people of Pine Ridge.

Katie's encounter with the newspeople hadn't been too inspiring, either. The moment they'd finished talking to the girls, Tammy and her crew seemed to forget them completely. One of the cameramen even accidentally knocked Katie over as he followed Tammy into the crowd to find more onlookers to interview.

If it hadn't been for her friends, Katie might have found the entire experience off-putting. Somehow she felt closer to them now than ever. The beautiful snow angel *had* appeared on top of their angel. That fact involved them with this angel. And while people seemed to be whipped up into a fever over the angel, Katie saw her friendship with Ashley, Christina, and Molly as a safe harbor, a circle of sanity, where she felt secure and comfortable.

She glanced around the room at her friends, who were also in her homeroom. They'd all received the same celebrity treatment when they arrived in school this morning. "They didn't sound crazy!" She defended them to Darrin.

"If you say so," Darrin sneered.

"They just believe in angels. So do I, really."

"No, you don't," Darrin scoffed in disbelief. "You're just saying that. You're too normal to believe crazy stuff like that."

Katie laughed. "Wow! You think I'm normal? I'm shocked."

"Ha!" He laughed back. "You only seem normal next to

your friends. Ashley made it sound like an angel would personally take you out on a trail ride if you came to the ranch this spring."

"She did not," Katie grumbled, turning away from Darrin.

When the buzzer for first class sounded, Katie joined her friends at the front of the room.

"See you guys later," Molly said sulkily. She dashed out the door as if she were dying to escape from them.

"I see she's still mad," Katie noted.

"She'll get over it," Ashley commented hopefully. "She said good-bye. That's a good sign." She turned to Christina. "Did you see Matt this morning?"

Christina rolled her eyes and sighed. "I saw him coming toward my locker, and I ran into the girls' room across the hall."

"What a mess!" Ashley sympathized. "You've got to talk to him soon and find out if he really likes you."

"I will," Christina agreed, "as soon as I figure out what I'm going to say."

Out in the hall, they joined the endless stream of kids going to class. Halfway down the corridor, Katie noticed Mrs. Gonzalez, the English teacher in charge of the yearbook, waving to her from a doorway. "See you later," she told her friends, and went to see what Mrs. Gonzalez wanted.

"Katie, I had a thought yesterday that I wanted to share with you," the tall, slim teacher said, pushing her long brown hair back from her shoulders. Her dark eyes shone with enthusiasm. Katie liked her. Although she let Katie run things herself, Mrs. Gonzalez was always thinking of ways to improve the yearbook and was always willing to lend a hand.

"I know that you like to take pictures to accompany the stories you do for the school newspaper, and it gave me this idea," Mrs. Gonzalez continued. "Why don't we have a yearbook feature about a day in the life of Pine Ridge?"

"I like the idea, but what would it be exactly?" Katie asked, not sure of what this would entail.

"There is a book out called *A Day in the Life of America*, and one called *A Day in the Life of Russia*. To create them, several photographers took pictures of different people, places, and things in each country, all in the course of one day. The books are very interesting, and they tell a lot about the two countries. I think it would be fun to do the same kind of thing here in Pine Ridge."

"But I'm only one photographer," Katie pointed out. "It would take me weeks to get enough pictures."

"We could assign some others," Mrs. Gonzalez suggested. "And perhaps we should make it a week in the life of the town instead of a day. Either way, I think it would be a great addition to the book."

"A lot better than Most Popular and Best Dressed," Katie agreed.

Mrs. Gonzalez wrinkled her nose in distaste. "Definitely."

Katie smiled at her. She was glad someone as intelligent as Mrs. Gonzalez agreed. Maybe this feature would offset the stupidity of the Mosts feature. She liked the idea.

"I'll bounce it off the kids at the staff meeting this afternoon if you like," Mrs. Gonzalez offered. "I first wanted to see if you liked the idea."

"I like it a lot," Katie agreed truthfully.

"Good. You'd better hurry to class now. See you after school."

With a nod and a wave, Katie rushed down the hall. Suddenly, she was excited about working on the yearbook again. She'd been so put off by the Most Popular page that she'd lost enthusiasm. Now she had it back again.

This was Katie's chance to do some serious photo-journalism. What would she find? Pine Ridge wasn't exactly a hotbed of interesting celebrities. Most of the people were pretty boring, in fact. And nothing exciting ever happened.

Just before stepping into her first class, Katie stopped outside the door. She'd been struck with a disturbing thought. What *would* she find when she set out with her camera?

What if all she found was boring people and no community spirit? Or, worse—what if she saw people being mean or dishonest?

Would she come away from this project feeling more hopeless about people than she already felt? Would it make her really sad?

It didn't matter, Katie decided with a wave of fresh resolve. If she planned to be a writer, she had to face things squarely and see them as they were. Even a fiction writer had to tell the truth about life, no matter how awful it might be.

She would go out into Pine Ridge and aim her camera with an unflinching eye. If her pictures exposed unpleasant truths about the town and its people—then so be it.

14

After school that day, Molly hurried out onto the icy pond. The fresh snow made it a bit hard to skate, but she didn't care. She had so much on her mind. She needed to be alone. To think.

As she turned and spun, her mind raced.

Why had that angel appeared? It was more than a fluke occurrence of nature. She was sure of that.

And what about the angel who'd helped get their car out of the ditch? Molly knew the policeman on the horse had to be an Officer Winger. The girls had gone to the bridge, and now, suddenly, there were signs of angel activity all around.

But how would it affect her? She'd asked for a way to help Liam, and she wanted Matt back. How would this angel help her with those things?

Molly spun in a tight circle, crossing her hands over her chest. As she turned, it came to her.

A party! A winter snow angel party!

She'd throw a huge winter bash and invite everyone in

school! If that didn't get her voted Most Popular, nothing would. Even kids who didn't like her would be impressed that she'd invited them. Even they would vote for her.

Yes! It was brilliant.

She'd invite Liam, too. The fun of a party might help bring him out of his shell. He'd be around happy people. It might make him feel happy again, as well.

Leaving the ice, Molly undid her skates, pulled on her boots, and hurried to her father's studio. If he okayed the party, her mother would surely go along.

When she got to the loft, she found her father working on his new painting with an almost feverish enthusiasm. His face was flushed as he jabbed at the canvas with his paintbrush. He was so involved that he didn't even appear to be aware that Molly had come into the room.

Liam also seemed—as usual—unconscious of his surroundings. Between her father's involvement in his work and Liam's blank, oblivious stare, Molly felt invisible.

She studied Liam with a straight-on boldness she'd have been too polite to use with someone who was aware of her. What was going on inside his head? Why had the flying geese affected him so deeply the other day?

"Molly." Her father spoke without turning. He had registered her presence, after all. "Your angel made the paper. It's on the table. Your name is even mentioned."

"My name?" she cried, hurrying to the table, where a newspaper lay folded among rolled tubes of oil paint.

Her father had left the *County Times* open to the story about the angel. It was only a column. It told how people were flocking to see this angel. Molly was given credit for building the original angel, along with Katie, Ashley, and Christina.

As Molly finished reading, Joy came running up the stairs. "Look at this!" she cried, waving a newspaper in the air.

At the top of the stairs she unfolded the paper so Molly and her father could see the front page. *"The National Tattler?"* Mr. Morgan asked with lifted brows. "Why are you reading that rag, Joy?"

"Look at this trash!" she cried impatiently.

"Oh, my gosh!" Molly cried.

A photo of the snow angel filled up the entire front page. "Amazing Miracle Angel!" blared the bright red headline. Inset in the lower right-hand corner was a picture of Molly with Ashley, Christina, and Katie.

Molly quickly flipped to the inside story. The first two paragraphs, telling about the angel, how it had been started by the girls and where it was located, were true enough. But after that the story became wild and unrecognizable to Molly.

"'Jets of fire shot out of the angel's eyes!'" she read, her voice rising incredulously. "'A crippled man was cured. A blind woman regained her sight.'"

She looked at her father with wide, bewildered eyes. "How can they write that when it's not true?"

Mr. Morgan chuckled bitterly. "The whole stock and trade of that paper and others papers like it is writing lies and half truths."

Molly read on. The story said she and her friends had made a circle around their smaller angel and then cried out for it to grow. Before their eyes it had grown. "That's a lie!" she cried, outraged.

Mr. Morgan took the paper from her and studied it. "I think I'll have my lawyer give these people a call," he said in a quiet, thoughtful voice. "I don't want you involved in this kind of sensationalism."

Molly chewed her lip, equally thoughtful. This kind of publicity might really boost her popularity in school. Now, at least, everyone would be aware of her. Once she gave the party, she'd be sure to be voted Most Popular.

"It's not such a bad thing," she disagreed with her father. "It's not hurting anyone."

"It's not helping anyone, either," her father replied, handing the paper back to her.

"Don't call your lawyer," Molly requested. "I don't think they'll put this in the paper again. They'll go on to something else. Don't you think so?"

"All right," Mr. Morgan agreed, sounding unconvinced. "As long as this is the only mention of it, I'll let it go."

"Mr. Morgan, I almost forgot. A package arrived this morning," Joy said.

"Ah! My paintings." Wiping his brush on a rag, he set it on the table. "I want to make sure there's no damage to them." He looked to Molly. "Would you stay here with Liam for just a moment while I check the paintings? If there's a problem, I don't want any time to pass before I call about it."

"Sure, Dad," she agreed.

Mr. Morgan left with Joy. Molly perused *The National Tattler* again, giving special attention to the photo of herself and her friends in the corner. *Do I look fat?* she wondered. *I do.*

With a horrified shiver, she realized this was her old, anorexic way of thinking. Why was it creeping back now?

"You don't look fat in that picture!" she scolded herself softly. "Stop thinking that."

Lowering the paper, she gazed at Liam. It seemed rude to just ignore him as if he weren't there—even though he probably wouldn't have noticed her attention.

Molly recalled a daytime soap she had followed while she was in the hospital recovering from anorexia. In it, the main character's brother had been in the hospital in a coma. The character, Julie, sat by his bedside talking to him all the time. Julie swore he could hear her even though he didn't respond. When he came out of the coma he said he'd heard her every word.

Maybe this was true of Liam, too.

Propping herself on the arm of his chair, Molly started telling Liam about the snow angel. He didn't respond in any way at all. His blue eyes stared, unmoving. His expression remained blank. She talked on, not knowing if he was even aware she was in the room.

"Since everyone is so excited about this angel," she explained, "I figured it would be a perfect theme for my party. Everyone's got angel fever, so why not go with it? After this article, everyone will be even more excited about it than they already are." She lifted the paper and held the front page out for him to see. "See? This is what she looks like."

As she lifted the paper in front of him, Liam turned away sharply.

"What?" Molly questioned, still holding up the picture. "It's just the snow angel. It won't hurt you."

"No!" he shrieked, his face contorting into lines of frantic terror. "Can't do it! Don't ask! Can't!"

Molly dropped the paper. "Do what? What, Liam?"

Tears fell from the boy's eyes, and he buried his face in his hands. "Can't . . . can't," he sobbed.

Molly put her hand on his heaving shoulder. "I'm sorry, Liam. What's the matter?"

He didn't respond, but only sat there with his face buried in his hands, trembling.

15

The next day, after school, Christina and Katie went to Children's House, as they usually did on Tuesday afternoons. The old Victorian house was close to the main Pine Ridge Hospital buildings, but it seemed worlds apart. For the sick children who stayed there, it was a much friendlier, less frightening place than the regular hospital. Volunteers like Katie and Christina made it even more pleasant by visiting, reading books, and just being there.

Katie used her fleece gloves to wipe the camera she wore around her neck as they climbed the stairs leading to the wraparound porch. "I'm glad you thought of this," she told Christina. "This is a great place to take some pictures for 'A Week in the Life of Pine Ridge.'"

"Thanks," Christina said as she kicked her boots on the steps to free them of snow.

Suddenly inspired, Katie leaped back down the stairs and aimed her camera at Christina standing on the porch.

Christina raised her hands in protest. "Don't take a picture of me."

"Put your hands down," Katie insisted. Christina put them down and Katie took the photo. "That's a great picture. There'll be three other kids taking pictures. This feature should be so good."

They went inside, took off their winter gear, and climbed the wide center stairway. On the stairs they met a petite woman with short, salt and pepper hair and bright, dark eyes. Ms. Baker ran the volunteer program at Children's House. "Hi, girls!" She greeted them warmly.

"Hi, Ms. Baker," they replied in unison.

"I hear there's a lot of excitement over at the ranch these days," she said.

"The cars haven't stopped coming," Christina reported. "It's really pretty crazy over there. Have you seen the angel yet?"

"Only in the papers. She looks gorgeous."

"She is," Katie confirmed.

"I'll have to get over there," Ms. Baker said. "You girls should check the day room when you go up. Some of the kids are doing a crafts project, and I think they could use some help."

"Okay," Christina said as she and Katie continued up the stairs. On the second floor, they went to a large, sunny room filled with child-sized tables and chairs.

Christina froze in the doorway. Matt Larson was standing at the table nearest the door, bent forward, helping a little boy make a building from craft sticks. "What do I do?" she asked Katie, her voice a frantic whisper.

"Don't do anything," Katie whispered back. "Just act natural."

Christina nodded sharply. Sure. That was the only thing to do. "Hi, Matt," she said in a voice that came out sounding falsely cheerful.

"Hi," he replied. Behind his glasses, his eyes looked anxious. Obviously, he felt as uncomfortable as she did.

Katie broke some of the tension by asking him to explain what they were doing with the craft sticks. "The kids are building whatever they'd like. Some of them are making boxes."

"I'm making one," a blonde girl named Elana volunteered, holding up a half-built box. "See! Christina, would you come help me with it?"

Christina was soon absorbed in helping the kids. Katie moved around the room snapping pictures of the children working. She loved being here around them. Their cheerfulness and determination to be well again were inspiring. Being here was certainly a temporary cure for Katie's dark thoughts about the mean, selfish nature of people. Being here lifted her spirits.

After taking a shot of two kids building together, Katie turned and found Matt standing behind her, looking anxious. "Can I talk to you a second?" he asked softly, shifting from foot to foot.

"Sure."

Matt drew her over into a corner of the room. "I guess you know Molly and I broke up," he began. Katie nodded. Matt shot a worried look in Christina's direction. "I'd really like to ask Christina to go out with me, but I'm not sure if it's the right thing to do. What do you think?"

"I have no idea," Katie replied with blunt honesty. "Molly answered the phone the day you called Christina. She thinks something's up between you two."

Matt grimaced. "What about Christina?" he asked. "Do you know how she feels?"

Again, Katie was honest and direct. "She'd love to go out with you. She likes you a lot. But she's not sure what to do because of Molly."

"But Molly and I have split up," Matt objected.

"Yeah, but Molly's not happy about it," Katie pointed out.

"Oh, she doesn't really care about me," Matt grumbled.

"She acts like she does. She was in tears the day you broke up," Katie told him.

Matt sighed. "I wish I didn't like Christina so much."

"Christina wishes she didn't like you, too," Katie said.

As they spoke, Christina looked up from the jewelry box she was helping a little girl construct. She stared right at Katie and Matt with questioning eyes, as if asking what they were talking about.

Suddenly uncomfortable with being in the middle, Katie lifted her camera to Matt. "I'd better get back to taking pictures," she said as an excuse to get away.

Matt asked what the pictures were for, and Katie told him about the yearbook feature. "I know where you should go," he said, his eyes lighting with an idea.

"Where?"

"The new soup kitchen and food pantry they just opened. It's called Come On Inn. That's a part of Pine Ridge people don't see."

"Good idea," Katie agreed enthusiastically. "I'd get a lot more interesting shots there than just taking the front of O'Herlihy's Food Market or the Pine Ridge Bike Shop."

"It's just two blocks from here, too," Matt added.

Ms. Baker walked into the room, staggering a bit under the weight of the cardboard box she carried. "Look at these," she said, smiling as she put the box down. Everyone crowded around to see. The box was filled with children's books for all ages, from picture books to novels. "There's a fortune in books here," Ms. Baker said happily.

"Where'd they come from?" Matt asked.

"I found them out on the porch," Ms. Baker replied. "There was no note. Nothing."

"Wow!" Christina murmured. "A mystery donor. That's awesome."

"It is," Ms. Baker agreed, her eyes bright. She dug more deeply into the box and pulled out a large yellow can. She looked at the front with a quizzical smile. "Canned yams," she said, turning the can in her hand. "Books and canned yams. That's a strange combination. Well, we can use both."

The kids clamored for the books. "I'll leave them here," Ms. Baker assured them. "There are enough books for everyone. I'll take the yams with me down to the kitchen."

A thoughtful look came to Ms. Baker's face. "In fact, there are more books here than even we need. There are even doubles of some books. I think I'll donate some to the homeless shelter over in Miller's Creek. There are always children in that shelter, and they'd enjoy these. I'll even throw in a few cans of yams."

"That's cool," Christina said. "It's like a gift that keeps giving."

"Something like that," Ms. Baker agreed.

Katie, Christina, and Matt helped Ms. Baker pack up some books to send over to the shelter. Matt went off with a volunteer to drive the books and yams over.

After they were done, Katie asked Christina to join her at the Come On Inn soup kitchen. Christina agreed on the condition that Katie tell her every word Matt said.

As they walked to the soup kitchen, following Matt's directions, Katie told all.

"This is so awful," Christina sighed. "I'm so confused. My horoscope says that my rising sign is in the house of love right now, so it's an excellent time for romance. But the tarot card reading didn't say anything about romance."

"You can't go by any of that stuff," Katie scoffed, as she always did when the subject arose.

"I don't want to argue about it," Christina said, waving Katie's objections away with a gloved hand. "You think what you like and so will I."

"Oh, all right," Katie gave in. "I guess you just have to decide who's more important to you, Matt or Molly."

"I can't decide that," Christina wailed.

They reached a low brick building that fit Matt's description. A handpainted sign over the door said "Come On Inn."

"This is it," Katie said, suddenly feeling nervous about entering. She'd never been in a soup kitchen before. What would it be like? What would the people be like?

"What's wrong?" Christina asked, sensing her distress.

"Just nervous, I guess," Katie admitted. With a toss of her head, she tried to throw off her anxiety. "Come on. Let's go in."

The moment they entered the plain room, Katie sensed something exciting was happening. "I can't believe this!" cried a heavyset woman with long brown hair. She stood beside five very large wooden crates. Several other women stood around her.

"Where did it all come from, Helen?" asked a tall, dark-haired woman.

"I don't know, Ruth," Helen said, tossing back a long black braid.

"You don't know?" Ruth questioned, aghast.

"Well, I know a delivery truck from Nature's Health over in Miller's Creek delivered them. But when I asked the driver who sent them, she told me that this morning, when the owner opened the shop, he found an envelope full of money. There was also a note with instructions to keep delivering five crates of food a week to the shelter for the rest of the year," Helen explained.

"This is great! So many people come in asking if we have baby food, and we never do," another woman said.

"You just gave me an idea, Yvonne," Helen told the woman. "We have more here than we can give away on pantry day. We can share this with the food pantry over in Fisher's Landing. They have several needy families with new babies. I'll go call the director there."

As Helen turned, she noticed Katie and Christina standing there. "And more volunteers, too!" she exclaimed, clapping her hands together in delight. "Wonderful! What a morning!"

"Umm, we're not really here to—" Katie began in a small voice.

Helen didn't seem to hear.

"Come with me," she said. "We were short-handed today, but now you're here. It's just a day of little miracles. You're just in time to help serve supper. What could be more perfect?"

Looking at one another helplessly, Christina and Katie knew they didn't have the heart to destroy this woman's happy, perfect day. With small shrugs, they followed Helen into the kitchen.

16

"Hello, Pine Manor Ranch," Ashley answered the phone in the office, located right off the living room. It was after school on Tuesday, and the phone had been ringing all afternoon. Ashley had volunteered to relieve her mother, who'd been taking the calls all day long.

"Sure, I can take your reservation for this spring," Ashley said to the woman caller. "You're coming all the way from Colorado. Wow! Oh, you heard about the snow angel. Yes, you heard right. Absolutely. Gee, no, we're completely booked for April. How about the end of May?"

Ashley took the customer's information and booked her into a room at the Pine Manor Inn for May. "Thanks for calling," she said, hanging up.

When she looked up, her tall, broad-shouldered father was standing in the doorway with an odd expression on his rough, weathered face. "Another reservation for May?"

"The very last opening in May," Ashley reported with a

triumphant grin. She noticed her father's pained expression. "You don't look very happy."

He scratched his sandy hair. "I'm a little concerned. Don't these folks realize the angel will have melted by spring?"

Ashley frowned. She hadn't thought of that. It could be a definite problem. "Maybe she won't melt," she suggested hopefully.

"Why wouldn't she melt?" Mr. Kingsley questioned skeptically.

Ashley shrugged. "Because she's special?"

"She's special, all right," Mr. Kingsley concurred. "But she'll probably melt."

"Even if she does melt, I think people will come to see the spot where she appeared," Ashley said, feeling confident she was right. "I know! If she melts, we could put up a white statue on the spot where she's standing. Like a kind of memorial to . . . The Miracle in the Snow!"

Her father winced. "Come on, Ashley, don't you think that's kind of crass and commercial?"

"So? Tammy Jacobs, the reporter, made up that name. I didn't."

"It doesn't matter. This angel is really affecting people deeply. I don't want to turn her into a moneymaking thing," Mr. Kingsley argued.

"But, Dad," Ashley protested. "She's already a moneymaker. The entire spring season is booked at the inn, and a lot of these people who are coming to see the angel now weren't even aware of the ranch before. Some of them are bound to come back again to rent horses and take trail rides and lessons."

"We didn't plan it that way," Mr. Kingsley protested. "It's not like we rigged this up just to bring in business."

"No, but what if she appeared at the ranch to help our business?" Ashley suggested. "What if that's the reason she's here?"

Mr. Kingsley frowned. "That never occurred to me. I don't know." He walked away, deep in thought.

As soon as he left, the phone rang again. "Hello, Pine Manor Ranch. How may I help you?"

"Ashley, it's me, Molly. I just had to talk to somebody."

"Sure, you can always talk to me," Ashley said, glad that Molly wasn't angry with all of them, as she'd seemed to be in school yesterday and today. "What's up?"

"The strangest thing happened with Liam yesterday, and I don't know what to think about it. I wanted to talk to you and Katie today, but every time I saw you, you were both with Christina."

"Molly, you really shouldn't be angry with Christina. She hasn't—"

"I don't want to talk about that now," Molly interrupted brusquely. "Tell me what you think about this." She went on to tell Ashley about how Liam had reacted when she showed him the picture of the snow angel. "By the time my father returned, he was calm again. I told Dad what had happened, but neither one of us understands it."

"Did you show him the picture a second time?" Ashley wondered.

"No. Dad thought it might be better not to upset him. They are both in the city today. Dad's taking Liam to some kind of psychiatrist who specializes in people who've suffered from severe traumas."

"Has anything else made Liam react like that?" Ashley asked.

"Just a flock of geese flying in the sky."

"Hmmm," Ashley considered. What did geese and angels have in common? "Wings!" she cried. "They both have wings."

"Wings," Molly repeated thoughtfully. "That's true. But why would that get such a reaction from him?"

"I have no idea," Ashley admitted.

"Me neither," Molly murmured. "Listen," she said, her voice brightening. "I want you to know that I'm having a huge winter party. I'm calling it the Snow Angel Winter Party. I'm inviting our entire class. What do you think?"

"It sounds fun. I guess that means Katie, Christina, and I are invited. So you're not mad anymore?"

"I wasn't really mad, not at you and Katie, anyway." She hesitated. "I think, though, that I've sort of been neglecting my old friends. I should see more of them, too."

Ashley didn't like the sound of this. Molly was always saying how her old friends had been such phonies. Why was she changing her mind about them now? "You are really mad, aren't you?" Ashley guessed.

"No, I'm not," Molly insisted in a defensive voice. "Things just aren't exactly the way I thought."

"What does that mean?" Ashley challenged.

"It means you three are tight and I'm still an outsider," Molly cried, her voice rising.

"That's not true," Ashley replied indignantly. "It's not fair, either. And, besides—"

"It doesn't matter." Molly cut her short, talking fast

and sounding almost tearful. "You're all still invited to the party. I've got to go." The phone clicked and she was gone.

Ashley stared at the phone in her hand a moment before hanging up. *Poor Molly*, she thought. *How awful she must feel.* Not only had she lost her boyfriend, but she thought she'd lost her best friends, too. How lonely!

Jeremy poked his head into the office. "Ashley, have you seen my remote control car, the one with the headlights that flash?"

"Aren't you a little old for stuff like that?" she asked.

"Yes!" he replied impatiently. "Some kids in school are putting a box of toys together for Children's House. They've been inspired by all the nice stuff happening in Pine Ridge lately. I want to join in."

"What nice stuff?" Ashley questioned.

"Somebody's mysteriously been delivering food to poor families and leaving brand-new clothes for the people over at the Miller's Creek homeless shelter. Stuff like that. Between that and the angel, people are feeling inspired to do good things for each other. It's like the good feeling is spreading all over town."

"Well, I don't know where your dumb old car is," Ashley snapped, turning away from him abruptly.

"Okay, okay," he said, backing away. "You don't have to be such a crab about it."

"Sorry," she mumbled. "I'm just not in a great mood." It was true. She suddenly felt very irritable.

Pulling on the winter jacket she'd tossed onto a chair, Ashley reached into the pocket and wrapped her hands protectively around the rectangular black remote control.

She refused to feel guilty. Look at all the good this angel was bringing—to everyone! She hadn't done anything wrong! She refused to believe she had.

Still gripping the remote tightly, she left the office and headed for the front door. Outside, a light snow had begun. She heard the sound of car engines and an occasional car horn. Out on the road, she saw the swirling red light on top of a Pine Ridge police car. The traffic jam was so massive and relentless in front of the ranch that the police had assigned a car to stay there and keep the flow of onlookers moving smoothly.

Glancing over the roof of the stable across from the house, Ashley noted that the sun was low in the sky. It seemed to sit right on the stable roof.

Good, she thought.

It was easier to see the angel's eyes flash when it was a little darker.

She squeezed the remote and headed down the snowy drive toward the angel. It was time for her daily miracle—the miracle of the remote-controlled flashing eyes.

17

The old man bent over the pot of soup and inhaled deeply. He shut his red-rimmed eyes and grinned a mostly toothless smile.

"It's good," Katie commented. "I tasted some."

The man pushed his plastic tray across the narrow table to her, and Katie filled his empty bowl with the steamy soup. "Thank you, sweetheart," the man said. "You're an angel."

Katie laughed. "No. No, I'm not."

With happy eyes, Katie glanced over at Christina, who'd been put in charge of dispensing soft rolls with a pair of long steel tongs. She was laughing with a tiny gray-haired woman in a heavy, worn jacket. Sensing Katie's gaze, Christina looked up and smiled back at her friend.

The people who had made their way to Come On Inn for a dinner of homemade chicken soup, a roll, salad, and a slice of apple pie weren't at all what Katie had expected. She'd thought they'd be a collection of miserable, unhappy souls, traipsing pathetically by. The idea of meeting such sad people had made her so uncomfortable, so nervous, that she'd had to force herself not to run away when Ruth announced they'd be opening the doors for supper.

In truth, some of the men and women who picked up trays and got into line for food were, indeed, sullen and wouldn't meet her eye. Others were even rude, complaining about the quality of the food and treating her like their servant. But the majority of people, especially the older ones, were pleasant and seemed appreciative. Many of them joked with her. Katie was surprised to find herself laughing and smiling so much while doing something she'd thought would be sad, even depressing.

"Hello there, little lady, what's in the pot tonight?" Katie found herself facing a wiry black man whose halo of white hair made him look like a dandelion just before it sends its seeds off into the breeze. His thoughtful face was deeply lined, and his dark eyes had a piercing quality to them, as though he could see past her face into her mind.

"Chicken soup," she replied with a smile. "It's good. Homemade."

"Yes, indeed," the man said, clapping his hands together. "Nothing better on a chilly day than homemade chicken soup. Lay some on me. These old bones need chicken soup."

Katie smiled at him and ladled the soup into his bowl.

The man put his tray down and enclosed her hands

in his own. "I know you're new here," he said warmly. "I'm Ogden A. Jones. Pleased to meet you."

"I'm Katie," she replied. "Pleased to meet you, too. What does the A. stand for?"

"Angel," he replied. "I'm part angel, just like you."

Katie laughed. "I'm not an angel."

The man cackled gleefully. "Me neither!" He laughed some more. "But my poor mama thought I was. Was she ever in for a shock!" His smile faded, and he stared at her with those searching dark eyes. "You're a deep thinker, aren't you, Katie?" he said.

Surprised by the comment, Katie was speechless a moment. "I . . . I don't know."

"You are. I can see it in your face. That's good. It's good to think deeply about things."

"I don't know. Sometimes I think it's a pain," Katie found herself saying, and she was surprised by her own words.

"Of course it's a pain," Ogden said. "Lots of things worth doing are painful. Don't you think a little seedling trying to work its way up through the dirt feels it's a pain to do all that work?"

"I don't know," Katie repeated. "Do plants feel?"

"Sure they do! That little seedling struggling in the dark doesn't know it's going to burst forth and be a great, gorgeous flower someday. While it's struggling, all it knows is the struggle."

"You think so?" Katie questioned.

Ogden tapped his forehead. "I know."

"Hey, Ogden, keep moving," a tall, carrot-haired woman with two preschool-age daughters scolded pleasantly from behind him. "My kids are hungry."

Ogden bowed slightly to the waiting woman. "Begging your pardon. I do tend to go on." He pushed his tray along the table, then turned back to Katie. "I'll see you next week."

"I don't know about that," Katie said as she ladled the steaming soup into bowls for the woman and her two daughters.

"Oh, you'll be here. I can tell," he insisted before heading on.

The tall woman thanked Katie for the soup. "Hi, I'm Heather. And I know you've met Ogden. He's a character, isn't he?" She smiled.

"He's nice," Katie replied.

"Yeah, he sure is," Heather agreed. "This whole place is nice. Ever since my husband died two months ago, things have been really tough for me and the girls. If it wasn't for this place, I don't know what we'd have done. After the mortgage is paid, I don't have a lot of money left for food."

Katie nodded. She felt so much sympathy for Heather and the other people she'd met today. She'd have liked to hear the story of everyone who came through. Why were they here? How had they gotten into such a tight spot that they couldn't even afford food?

"Could I take your picture later?" Katie asked. She quickly explained what it was for.

"I'd rather you didn't," Heather declined. "I don't feel good about this. I mean, I'm grateful, but I wish I didn't have to be here. I don't want my kids to be embarrassed, either."

"Sure, I understand," Katie said, feeling bad for even asking.

Katie's attention was diverted by Helen, who hurried across the room to greet a young woman with a long black braid pushing a bundled up, red-cheeked baby in a rickety, faded-blue stroller. "Rosa, I'm so glad you came," she heard Helen say to the woman. "We got a surprise shipment that will interest you, and I didn't want you to have to wait for Food Pantry Friday. I'm sure you can use this now."

Katie had learned that although Come On Inn served supper every afternoon, they only gave out food on Fridays. On Friday mornings people came in and received the food that had been donated by church organizations and local stores.

Helen ushered Rosa and her baby into a back room and closed the door. Katie was sure Helen was giving the young woman some of the mysterious jars of baby food.

The line of people had stopped, giving Katie a chance to look around. Ogden was at a table in the far corner of the room, making everyone around him laugh as they ate. Heather and her daughters had joined him there. Even the little girls were giggling at whatever Ogden was saying.

It would have been a great picture, Katie thought. But she couldn't take it now. Not after what Heather had said. Putting herself in the woman's place, Katie knew she'd feel the same way. In a way, she'd had to depend on the kindness of strangers after her parents died. Luckily, the strangers turned out to be warm and loving people. Katie thought about the comparison. She realized that she had more in common with these people than she first thought.

In a few minutes, Rosa and Helen emerged from the room, each carrying a large brown bag. They set the bags down beside the stroller. Rosa lifted the baby from the stroller and handed her to Helen. Together, they walked toward the food line.

"Thank you so much for the extra bag of food," Rosa said to Helen. She picked up a tray, bowl, and utensils. "My neighbor will be so glad to have these jars of food for her babies. Those twin boys of hers eat so much! And thank you for the canned yams. I know she'll appreciate those."

"Good," said Helen. "The day before yesterday I found a whole crate of them on the doorstep when I opened up. I don't know where they came from, either, but they're good. I ate a can myself just to be sure. They've got honey baked into them. Very delicious."

Katie's jaw dropped slightly when Helen mentioned the yams. Yams? Again? Just like at Children's House. Glancing at the bags near the stroller, she saw a yellow can of yams peeking from the top of Rosa's bag. They were the same brand.

"I'm sure my neighbor will love them," Rosa told Helen as she tied the baby's warm wool hat under her pudgy chin.

"Tell her to come down," Helen prodded as she cooed to Rosa's smiling, toothless baby.

Rosa shook her head. "She's too proud. Too ashamed to have to ask for help. I'm proud, too, but the baby has to eat, and ever since the man José and I worked for closed his business, we've had trouble finding work. My neighbor worked for the same man, so she's hurting, too. I never thought of bringing food to her. It's so heavy to carry extra. But if someone can give this food, I can surely carry some extra."

Katie smiled at Rosa as she poured her some soup. Here this woman had so little, and she was bringing extra baby food home for a needy neighbor. She'd been inspired by someone else's generosity to be generous herself.

Katie was struck with an idea. Did one kind act produce another kind act, and another, and another? Like a chain reaction, or a line of dominoes?

"Do you live far?" she impulsively asked Rosa.

"About ten blocks from here. Why?" Rosa asked as she picked up her tray.

"I heard what you were saying about carrying the extra food. I see you have the baby and all. I could help you carry it."

"No, thank you . . . but . . ." She glanced back at the stroller and the two overflowing bags. "Well, I suppose I'd better accept. I'll never be able to carry both of these bags and push the stroller." She smiled gratefully at Katie.

"You can go any time," Helen told Katie. "Supper will be slow from now on."

"When you're done eating, let me know," Katie told Rosa. She glanced down at her nearly empty pot of soup. "I'd better go into the kitchen and get more in case anyone wants seconds," she said. Grabbing both steel handles, she carried the pot toward the kitchen. Ogden caught her eye and waved to her. Katie nodded back happily and began humming a lively song she'd heard on the radio that morning. She hadn't felt so lighthearted in a long time.

18

"I can't believe this," Alice fumed as she impatiently tapped the truck's steering wheel. Christina and Katie had made it back to the hospital just as Alice was pulling up. They'd dropped Katie off at home, but now they were caught in a traffic jam as they tried to get back to the ranch.

Seated beside her mother, Christina peered out the front window at the row of idling cars, their mufflers sending up clouds of white smoke, their red brake lights flickering on and off as they slowly crawled forward. All these people wanted to see the angel. Christina noticed that the car in front of theirs had an out-of-state license plate. The news of the angel was spreading fast.

"It's dark out, for heavens sake!" Alice cried. "Don't these people have to get home? Don't they have lives to attend to?"

"They are attending to their lives," Christina said quietly.

"What do you mean?" Alice asked.

"Isn't it more important to attend to your spirit than to your . . . I don't know . . . to your supper?" Christina replied. "Mom, what do you think of the angel?"

Alice sighed and sat back in her seat, resigned to waiting out the traffic jam. "Honestly, I don't know what to think. I don't believe she's just a fluke of nature, but I don't know why she's here."

"I think she's here to give people hope," Christina offered sincerely. "I think she's a sign that we shouldn't give up."

"Give up what?" Alice challenged her to be more exact.

Christina had to think about that a moment. "The angel wants us to know that it's still important to be kind," she ventured. "You know, that even though the world seems harsh sometimes, it doesn't mean we should be harsh ourselves."

"But who sent her?" Alice asked as she moved the truck forward a few feet.

"The angels," Christina answered without hesitation.

"Why didn't the angels come themselves, then?" She asked Christina.

"They do come, all the time," Christina answered. "But people don't always realize they've been touched by an angel. This time I think the angels wanted everyone to see them."

"What about those flashing eyes?" Alice asked. "What's that all about?"

"I think it's proof for people who want to rationalize that the wind and snow whipped the angel together. It's a small miracle."

"Maybe," Alice conceded.

Finally, they reached the front gate. There they saw Mr. Kingsley hanging a rope across the front entrance. "That's all for tonight, folks," he told the people. "Sorry. Come back tomorrow if you like." He spotted Alice and Christina and opened the rope to let them through.

"How come she gets in?" a man shouted angrily, stretching his head out the window.

"She lives here," Mr. Kingsley replied firmly.

As they drove past the angel, they saw crowds surrounding her, standing in the snow, seeming not to care about the cold. A group stood in a cluster holding candles. Others shone flashlights on her. All they wanted was to be near her.

"This is craziness, though," Alice commented.

"I don't agree," Christina said. "I think it's a wonderful thing. And there's more to it, Mom. Someone has been going around Pine Ridge doing kind things, donating books and food."

"Who do you think that is?" Alice asked.

"The angel," Christina murmured.

"Christina," her mother scolded skeptically. "Really."

"I do think it!" Christina insisted. "It all started at the same time the angel appeared. And it's setting off a reaction. People are catching the spirit. They're sharing what they get."

"That's wonderful, but do you actually think the snow angel moves around and does these things?"

Christina nodded. "You saw her eyes flash the other day. What I really think is that every time her eyes flash, a good deed is performed."

"I don't know," Alice said warily.

"I do," Christina said firmly. "I just know it's true."

When Alice pulled up in front of their house, Christina noticed an unfamiliar car parked nearby. As they climbed out of the truck, a woman got out of the car. "Hi, I'm Liz Parker," she introduced herself. "I'm writing an article for the *Miller's Creek Courier*. I'd like to interview you about the angel."

"I'm sorry, but no," Alice said, moving briskly past the woman.

"But I've been waiting out here for an hour," the woman protested.

"I'm sorry, no," Alice repeated as she pulled open her front door.

"But, Mom," Christina spoke up. "Why not?"

With a firm hand, Alice ushered Christina through the front door. "Because we've had enough publicity on this." She turned to the woman. "Sorry, Ms. Parker. We can't do it."

Once the door was closed, Christina held her mother in a disapproving scowl. "Why shouldn't people hear how we feel about the angel?"

"Because you may think you're sure of some things, but I'm not as sure," Alice replied adamantly. "I don't want to influence people or say things I'm not certain of. Let people make up their own minds."

"Then why can't I talk?" Christina argued. "I don't feel the same about it as you."

"Because you're only thirteen, and I'm your mother," Alice replied. "I don't want you talking to the press at thirteen." She pulled off her woolen cap and yanked off her gloves. "I'm tired and I want to go take a shower, so we'll talk about this some more later."

Shrugging off her coat, she tossed it on the couch and headed toward her bedroom.

Christina stood, staring for a moment at the spot where her mother had been, still arguing with her in her mind. Then she turned and looked out the window.

Liz Parker still sat in her car with the inside light on. She was looking down at something as if she were reading or writing.

Impulsively, Christina ran back out. Why should she be quiet about something she felt so deeply about? The woman didn't notice her as she came around the front of the car to the driver's-side window. She rapped on the window, and Liz Parker looked up sharply. After her second of surprise passed, she rolled down the window, looking at Christina expectantly.

"I'll talk to you," Christina said.

"Excellent. Thank you," Liz said as she leaned across the seat and opened the passenger door. "Come on in."

Christina sat beside the woman.

"Let me ask you something," Liz began. "You live here, so you would know. Is this the first time you've witnessed anything, uh, otherworldly going on?"

Christina pressed her fingertips together a moment. She looked back at the house and saw the light go on in the bathroom window. She didn't have a lot of time to talk. How much could she tell, *should* she tell?

They didn't want the ranch and the woods ruined, but it had already happened. The snow angel was bringing more people every day. And although it was creating a traffic problem at the ranch, it wasn't doing real harm. It was doing good, in fact. People were catching the spirit of goodness.

"Yes," she told Liz. "You could definitely say there's been angel stuff going on here for a while."

"Really?" Liz asked, impressed. "Where? How?"

"In the woods," Christina said. "This woods has many power spots, places where good energy collects. I can't tell you exactly where, but there's a spot in the woods where I've seen angels."

There. She'd done it. She'd told about the angels, or begun to.

Christina glanced at Liz Parker for her reaction.

The reporter simply stared back at Christina, looking stunned but happy, as if she'd just won the lottery.

19

"What an idiot," Molly grumbled as she sat cross-legged on the floor of her father's painting studio with the *Miller's Creek Courier* spread across her lap. It was Thursday, and Molly had come up to the studio after school to be near Liam.

Liam sat draped across the armchair behind her. His hand dangled listlessly over the arm as he gazed blankly out the window at the gently falling snow.

His visits to Dr. Andrews, the psychiatrist he'd been seeing all week, seemed to have tired him. Or maybe he was depressed by them. Molly couldn't tell, but he seemed even more withdrawn than ever.

Molly thought about her conversation with her father that morning. "Dr. Andrews thinks Liam is close to a breakthrough, but something is holding him back," Mr. Morgan had explained. "He's convinced Liam blames himself for the accident and that's why he's withdrawn."

Mr. Morgan shook his head sadly. "I can't understand

why Liam would feel that way. He had nothing to do with the accident. But every time the doctor tries to make Liam understand that, the boy seems to drift further away. I'm not sure he'll ever fully recover."

Molly had looked at her father thoughtfully. She knew there must be a way to reach Liam, and she was more determined than ever to find it.

She snapped out of her thoughts and stared down at the paper on her lap. Christina's face in a black-and-white photo smiled back up at her. Above Christina were the words, printed in large, bold type: LOCAL GIRL REVEALS AMAZING SECRET OF ANGELS, by Elizabeth Parker.

How could she do that? Molly wondered. They'd agreed not to tell the world about the angels. Sure, she hadn't said anything about the bridge, but she might as well have. The woods would be swarming with people now. "Idiot," Molly grumbled again as she frowned at Christina's photo.

"Who's an idiot?" Mr. Morgan asked from the other side of the room as he cleaned his paintbrushes with a large turpentine-soaked rag.

That afternoon he'd finished a painting of the family castle in Ireland. Molly liked it a lot. The medieval castle loomed dark in shades of purple and blue, while behind it a yellow and pink sky blazed with shards of white light that bounced off the castle's leaded windows. It was very dramatic.

"My friend—former friend—Christina Kramer is an idiot," she replied impatiently. "She told this newspaper all about the angels in the woods. Then she went on and on about all the things she believes. Things like tarot cards and horoscopes and crystal healing."

"Is that bad?" her father inquired.

"It makes her sound nutty."

"Do you think she's nutty?" Mr. Morgan asked.

"No, but when you read what she says, it makes her sound like a total flake. Other people will think she's nutty."

"Maybe she doesn't care," Mr. Morgan suggested.

"You're right, she probably doesn't," Molly agreed. Christina was strong that way. She was who she was, no matter what. Grudgingly, Molly had to give her credit for that—although she didn't feel like giving Christina credit for anything at all.

This week she'd spoken to Ashley and Katie, but she had avoided Christina. Molly no longer sat with them at lunch or chatted in front of their lockers before and after school. Unfortunately, she had discovered that her old friends weren't that willing to just take her back, either. They'd continued their lives without her, and now there didn't seem to be a place for her in their crowd anymore.

Without Matt to fall back on when no one else was around, the way she'd always done, it had been a truly lonely week.

Once she told everyone about the snow angel party, all that would change. She was confident of that. Now the most important thing was to finish making the plans and invite everyone. That would send her popularity soaring, and her old friends would welcome her back. She just had to finish writing up a few more invitations tonight, and she'd give them all out tomorrow.

Molly looked up at Liam. She had spent countless hours since his arrival imagining how he'd be if he were normal. Handsome, maybe even fun to be with. Would he ever snap out of this?

"Watching you paint doesn't seem to be helping Liam much," she said to her father, closing the newspaper. "It's not upsetting him or making him happy or anything."

"I know," Mr. Morgan agreed unhappily. "He was extremely agitated by it in Ireland. He would move about, and his eyes were so full of expression that I expected him to speak at any moment, although he didn't. I was so sure he'd have a breakthrough if he stayed with me."

Molly stood. An idea had suddenly occurred to her. "What were you painting while you were in Ireland? The castle?"

"No," he replied. "See for yourself." He nodded at a large sheet that covered several canvases. "Those are some of the paintings I did," he said.

Molly went to the pile and began to carefully lift one corner of the sheet. "Just pull it off," her father suggested. "The paint is dry. You can't harm them."

Molly eagerly threw back the sheet. There were three paintings facing away from her.

"Oh, my gosh," she whispered as she turned one of the paintings around and saw its subject.

"What is it?" Mr. Morgan asked.

Looking up, Molly noticed that Liam was facing in her direction. His gaze was so unfocused, she couldn't be sure if he was looking at her, exactly, but maybe he was. Slowly she turned the painting around so he would be able to see it.

It was a painting of an angel. A majestic green-and-gold angel with windswept red hair walking barefoot along the rocky coast of an Irish seashore, her robes flowing behind her.

Molly breathed deeply, holding in her breath as she waited for Liam to react.

At first, Liam didn't even seem to notice it. But then, he began to squirm in the chair.

"Molly, what's going on?" Mr. Morgan asked anxiously.

"No!" Liam shouted. "I can't do it! Don't ask! I can't!"

"He's talking!" Mr. Morgan gasped as he stared at Liam. "What does it mean?"

"I can't. I'm sorry! I can't!" Liam wailed.

Molly turned the picture away from him, leaning it blank-side up against the wall. Filled with compassion for the quaking boy, she went to his side and put her arms around him. He sobbed into her shoulder.

Her father came to her side and put his hand soothingly on the back of Liam's neck. "I don't understand," he said to Molly.

"I don't either," Molly admitted. "But it's something about the angels. Are all those paintings of angels?" Her father nodded. "That's what's getting to him. Dad, you have to start painting angels again."

"But look how upset it's made him."

"Upset is better than nothing, isn't it? You said so yourself," Molly replied as Liam's shaking lessened and he drew away, turning his face into the chair.

"I don't know what to do," Mr. Morgan said. "I'll call

the doctor and ask. I simply don't know."

Molly felt she knew, though. She knew that the angel was the key to bringing Liam back from whatever deep and private terror tormented him. "Maybe we should take him to see the snow angel," she suggested. "Yes. I definitely think we should."

20

"Molly, I have a great idea," Katie said the next day in school when Molly handed her the invitation to her party.

"What?" Molly asked.

"Why don't you make this party a fundraiser for the new food pantry? Everyone who comes has to bring a can of food. Then we'll get all the cans and bring them over to Come On Inn." She went on to tell Molly how she and Christina had accidentally become involved with the soup kitchen and food pantry project. "It was a great place," Katie added. "I met this really neat old guy named Ogden, and a bunch of nice people run it."

Molly considered it. "I suppose everyone can spare one can of food."

"Sure they can," Katie agreed. "How many kids have you invited?"

"Two hundred."

"Two hundred!" Katie gasped. "That's awesome."

"But I didn't write anything about a fundraiser on the invitation," Molly pointed out.

"That's okay, we can tell kids to tell other kids."

"I guess," Molly agreed, although she wasn't convinced that would work. "Katie, I was wondering, when will you hold the elections for Most Popular and all that?"

"There are ballots in today's *Writer*," she replied, referring to the school paper she wrote for. "All the nominations have to be in by the end of next week. Why?"

"I was hoping to be named . . . something," Molly admitted, looking away self-consciously.

"That's so dumb," Katie blurted. "What did you want to be named?"

"I don't know. Most Popular, maybe."

Katie stared at her in disbelief. She'd thought Molly was above that kind of thing. "What difference does it make if you're voted Most Popular or not?"

"I'd just like it, that's all," Molly said, a bit coldly.

Katie shrugged. She'd decided this contest was something she would just never understand. "Whatever. But what do you think of my idea about the cans?"

Molly walked to the tall trash can that stood at the end of the locker bank and dumped all the invitations inside.

"What did you do that for?" Katie cried.

"I love your idea," Molly said. "And I'm inviting the entire school. I'll put up a sign and tell everyone to bring two cans of food. They can spare it."

"Cool!" Katie said. She'd call Helen tonight and tell her the food would be coming. Katie knew what she'd bring—two cans of corned beef hash. Aunt Rainie had a closet full. "But will your parents mind?"

"No," Molly replied confidently. "I just asked if I could have a huge party and they agreed. I didn't say how many kids I'd be inviting."

"Very cool," Katie said.

"What did you think of Christina's interview in the *Miller's Creek Courier*?" Molly asked in a sarcastic voice.

"I wish she hadn't done it," Katie admitted. "Things are crazy enough over there. But it's a free country." Katie leaned in closer. "Her mother was furious. She'd told her not to talk to the reporter."

"At least Alice has some sense," Molly said smugly.

"You shouldn't be so mad at Christina," Katie said. "She's barely talked to Matt since you guys broke up. It's not her fault he likes her."

"I don't want to talk about this," Molly said as the buzzer for first class sounded. "See you later."

Katie watched Molly go. She seemed so unhappy. Katie knew Molly couldn't feel good about this fight with Christina. She and Christina had been so close. Katie wished there was some way she could make Molly understand that she had nothing to be angry about.

Shrugging off the disturbing thought, Katie walked toward her first class. Along the way, she thought about "A Week in the Life of Pine Ridge."

The other day, before leaving the food pantry–soup kitchen, she'd taken a photo of the outside. She'd thought no one would be in the picture, but, unexpectedly, Ogden had come out the door as she was snapping the photo. "I'm sorry," she apologized. "I took your picture by mistake."

"No problem," he told her, smiling. "I'm proud of this place."

"Then you don't mind being seen here?" Katie questioned, mentally contrasting his reaction with Heather's. "I wanted this photo for my school yearbook." She explained the project.

"Not a bit. Shame isn't in my vocabulary. Life knocks us all around at one time or another. If you're lucky, someone helps you. No shame in that. One way or another, everybody takes their lumps in life. You can use old Ogden A. Jones in your picture. Not a problem."

"Thanks," Katie had told him, knowing her photo would be more interesting with his oddly fascinating face in it.

Now she had another great idea. She'd photograph the snow angel with all the people surrounding her. It was certainly something unique to Pine Ridge, and it would make a really interesting photo.

She decided to go over to the ranch right after school.

21

Mesmerized by its beauty, Christina stared up into the beautiful face of the snow angel. Just looking at the angel filled her with a deep inner happiness. It didn't matter that her mother was still angry with her for talking to Liz Parker against her wishes. She felt the world should know about this miraculous angel. In her heart, Christina was sure she'd done the right thing.

The crowd was thicker than ever. Behind her, a man was selling T-shirts with a photo of the snow angel silkscreened on the front. Another man had created postcards from a photo of the angel. Both seemed to be doing a brisk business.

"Look at this," complained Ashley, coming alongside Christina. "Those guys are making a fortune, and my parents refuse to do even a bumper sticker."

Christina turned to her. "A bumper sticker?"

"Sure. It would say Pine Manor Ranch. Riding. Lessons. Boarding. Famous Home of the Snow Angel. And then the phone number. Good idea, huh?"

"I suppose," Christina replied absently. She didn't object to the idea. But she couldn't understand how Ashley could be thinking about advertising the ranch when a real miracle was sitting in the pasture on her very own property. "Have her eyes flashed today?" she asked.

"Um, no. That reminds me," Ashley replied.

"Reminds you of what?"

Ashley colored ever so slightly.

"What?" Christina pressed.

"Oh, nothing," Ashley said. "I mean, it reminded me that her eyes haven't flashed." She giggled nervously.

Christina fixed her in a hard stare. What was making her so anxious? "Is everything okay?" she inquired.

"Of course!" Ashley gazed around at the crowd. "I just wish my parents would let me do the bumper sticker. Look at all the free advertising we're passing up. It makes me nuts to think about it."

"Let them worry about it," Christina advised. It had always seemed to her that Ashley worried too much about the finances of the ranch. She was only thirteen, after all. What could she actually do? But, then, Ashley had always seemed older than her years.

"I can't let them worry about it," Ashley snapped. "They make a mess of it."

"Okay, Ashley, lighten up," Christina said, offended by Ashley's impatient tone. What *was* the matter with her? She wasn't usually this tense.

"Easy for you to say," Ashley muttered, walking away.

As Christina watched Ashley walk over to the T-shirt salesman and begin talking to him, someone put a hand lightly on her shoulder. She turned to face white-haired Mrs. O'Herlihy. "Christina, dear, I read your interview in the *Courier.* I was very interested in the part where you said every time the angel's eyes flash a good work is done."

"Thank you."

"How did you discover this?" Mrs. O'Herlihy inquired, dropping her voice to a confidential whisper.

"It's just an idea I had," Christina admitted, feeling suddenly self-conscious about how little backing this concept had. It was a nice idea that had popped into her head, but she had no real grounds for believing it.

"Oh," Mrs. O'Herlihy said in a disappointed voice. "Then the angel didn't speak to you or anything like that?"

"Oh, no," Christina gasped. "I didn't want to give that impression. It was only a nice thought I had."

Mrs. O'Herlihy pressed her lips together thoughtfully. Then she spoke. "You see . . . what I wanted to know was . . ." She leaned even closer. "A couple came into our market this afternoon with three small children. They seemed sort of down on their luck—you know, shabby. When I rang up their bill, they were five dollars short. Normally, I would have had them put some items back, but this time I thought of the angel and I said, 'Oh, just pay me when you can,' and let them have the things."

Christina was impressed. The O'Herlihy family, who ran O'Herlihy's Market in town, were known more for their sour dispositions than for their generosity. "That was very nice of you," she commented.

"I was wondering if . . . if the angel's eyes flashed

around one o'clock. That's when I did it," Mrs. O'Herlihy blurted.

"I don't know. I was in school then," Christina told her.

"Oh, that's right," Mrs. O'Herlihy said. "I'll have to find someone who was here around one. Excuse me. Maybe that salesman's been here all day."

"I bet they did flash and no one saw," Christina called after her, wanting her to feel she'd been rewarded for her kindness.

An excited murmur swelled up among the crowd. Christina saw that they were all staring up at the angel. She looked up, too, and saw its eyes flashing.

A joyful feeling filled her. Somewhere, some act of kindness had just been performed. It had to be.

The angel had transformed Pine Ridge. People just couldn't do enough to be kind to one another.

"Someone has just made the angel happy!" a dark-haired woman cried out. "Human kindness is overflowing."

The crowd murmured its agreement. A ripple of soft applause sounded. Obviously a lot of people had read Liz Parker's article. Christina's idea had caught on.

She caught sight of Molly and her father making their way toward the angel with Liam between them. Although she'd never seen Liam, she knew this must be him from Molly's description. He was better looking than she'd expected. Very good-looking, in her opinion. Too bad he was in such a bad state.

She smiled and waved, but Molly either didn't see her or pretended not to. Hurt, Christina drew her hand back.

In the next moment, she saw Liam pull back as if he

wanted to run away. His eyes were wild with terror. What was going on?

Christina headed toward them to see if she could help, but before she reached them, Molly and Mr. Morgan had whisked Liam back into the chauffeur-driven limo. She saw only the broad back of their chauffeur as he helped them return to the backseat.

The chauffeur turned and stared at the angel a moment. He shot the snow sculpture a quick smile before rounding the car and disappearing inside.

How strange, Christina thought. What had just happened?

She searched the crowd for Ashley, wanting to ask if she'd seen the incident with Liam. Ashley was hurrying away from the angel, back toward her house.

Christina hurried through the snow to catch up with Ashley. "Wait up," she called, but Ashley kept going.

"Can't," she called back. "I have homework."

Christina quickened her pace. Why wouldn't Ashley stop to talk to her? What was going on with Ashley, anyway? She seemed too weird. She decided to check Ashley's horoscope when she got home. Maybe some difficult planet, like Mars, had shifted somewhere in her chart.

"Ashley!" Christina called, breaking into a run once they were on the drive. "What's the rush?" she asked breathlessly when she caught up to her.

"Homework. I told you."

Christina took hold of Ashley's arm. "Is something bothering you?" she asked.

"No!" Ashley wrenched her arm away angrily.

"What is it?" Christina asked.

"You!" Ashley said angrily.

"Me?" Christina couldn't believe what she was hearing.

"Yeah. Why did you have to say all those things about the angel in that article? Why did you have to say her eyes flash when someone does something good?"

"What do you care?" Christina challenged. "You wanted the publicity."

"But why did you have to say *that*?" Ashley shot back.

"Because it seemed like it might be true."

"You're always saying this crazy stuff, Christina!" Ashley shouted. "It's one thing to believe it, but it's another thing to say it to a newspaper. Now everyone believes it. I heard them all talking just now! What a laugh! They're all doing good things to make her eyes flash."

"Is that so terrible?" Christina asked.

"But it's just something you made up—as if you even know what you're talking about." Ashley's eyes brimmed with tears. "I can't talk about this! I'm going!"

She turned abruptly. "Ashley!" Christina cried, pulling on her arm to stop her from leaving.

The unexpected tug threw Ashley off balance. She pitched forward, and her foot slid on a small patch of ice. With flailing arms, she careened onto the ground.

"Oh, Ashley, I'm so sorry!" Christina lunged forward to assist her friend. "I didn't mean to."

"Leave me alone!" Ashley said, yanking her arm away and slowly climbing to her feet.

Christina was completely bewildered. Why was Ashley so angry about what she'd said?

As Ashley stormed away, Christina noticed a black rectangular object lying in the snow right where Ashley had fallen. Bending, she picked it up and wiped the snow from it.

A remote control. But it wasn't for a TV or a VCR. It was too small for that. She lifted her head and gazed at Ashley's back as she marched away from her through the snow. This had fallen from her pocket when she fell.

Why was she carrying the remote to some kind of toy around with her? Surely that's what this was—the remote to a toy truck, car, or plane. It had only two buttons, on and off.

Christina's pulse quickened, and a horrible nausea swept over her. "No," she whispered as a terrible thought came to her. "She wouldn't."

Yet the suspicion persisted, and Christina had to know the truth.

Slowly turning, she put the remote control into her pocket and headed back toward the snow angel. The pounding of her heart seemed to thunder in her ears.

Don't let it be true! Don't let it be true! she chanted silently as she walked to the base of the angel.

Pulling in a long, shaking breath, she held down the button on the right side of the remote.

"Look!" cried the woman standing behind her. "The eyes!"

They were flashing.

"Somewhere, someone's done something wonderful!" a man shouted. "The angel is happy."

Christina pushed the off button. The eyes stopped flashing. The eyes were controlled by the remote! Ashley had set this up! She'd been controlling the eyes all along!

Running as fast as she could away from the angel, Christina finally staggered to one of the posts supporting the split level fence. She leaned heavily on it, trying to slow her breathing, trying not to let the overwhelming nausea she felt get the best of her.

22

On Saturday morning, Katie climbed off the bus in the downtown part of Pine Ridge. It was really no more than a main street lined with low brick buildings, but it was the busiest part of town.

She adjusted the strap of the camera around her neck and gazed around. It was only nine in the morning, and everything was pretty quiet. Many of the stores were just now opening.

"Hello, there, my friend," came a familiar voice. Katie turned and faced Ogden. "Looking for more photos that reveal the inner soul of Pine Ridge?" he asked.

"Yes," Katie said with a smile. She wouldn't exactly have expressed it that way, but that was what she was doing.

"Mind if I trail along?" he asked.

"I guess not. But I'm warning you it might be boring."

"Naw," Ogden disagreed. "Nothing bores me."

"Nothing?" Katie asked skeptically.

"Nope. I consider myself a student of life, so everything interests me."

Katie stopped to take the picture of a store owner shoveling last night's light snowfall from the front of his shop. When he noticed her lining up the shot, he smiled and posed next to his shovel.

"Being a student of life must make things pretty interesting," Katie noted as they moved on down the street.

"You should know," Ogden replied. "Isn't that what you are, after all?"

"Me?"

"Sure. What else is a writer and photographer?"

Katie considered the question for a moment. "I suppose you're right. I never thought of it that way."

Katie liked Ogden. She felt comfortable with him, but there was more to it than that. He made her feel self-confident and good about who she was, more so than usual. She even felt more energetic around him.

"Were you always a student of life?" she asked. It was her way of trying to find out more about him. Had he always been as down on his luck as he appeared to be now?

Ogden tilted his head thoughtfully. "I believe I was. Of course, now that I have more time to myself, life is easier to study."

Katie stooped to take a picture of a black cat sitting in front of a store sunning herself in a patch of warm light. "What kind of job did you have?"

"I was a cook."

Katie looked up at him, impressed. Although he wasn't young, he didn't seem old enough to be retired. "What happened? Did you get fired?"

"Fired myself," Ogden said proudly. "I needed more time to be a student of life."

Katie nodded. Many times she'd heard her Uncle Jeff complain about people who didn't work. "Plain lazy," he'd mumble. It sounded as though Ogden would probably fall into that category, at least according to Uncle Jeff.

Katie didn't think it was right not to work. But she liked Ogden so much. She didn't know what to think. Besides, who was she to criticize? It wasn't her business.

Still, she had to know. "Doesn't it bother you that you have to eat at places like Come On Inn?"

"I don't have to," he replied, unruffled by the question.

"You don't?" Katie asked.

"The way I see it, nobody has to do anything they don't want to do."

"But you'd starve if you didn't," Katie pointed out.

"Then that would be my choice."

"But why don't you look for another job?" Katie asked.

"Then I'd have less time to be a student of life," Ogden replied.

"Can't you be a student of life and work, too?"

"Why should I if I don't have to?"

Katie sighed. She still believed working and making your own money was the right thing to do. "It's your life, I suppose," she conceded.

"Sure is." Ogden smiled. His dark eyes brightened with an idea. "Come on. I know where you can get a great shot."

Leading the way, he hurried down the street until they came to the small Pine Ridge Library. Walking inside, they saw a group of young children sitting in a circle with books on their laps. From their appearance, Katie could tell they had Down's syndrome.

"They look sort of bored," she commented. "But it might be an interesting picture."

"They are bored. I'll make it a better picture. Wait a minute." Ogden hurried to the woman sitting nearby, who seemed to be in charge. He spoke to her quickly. The woman seemed worried at first, but Ogden quickly charmed her and she nodded, agreeing to something.

Ogden jumped into the middle of the circle. "Good morning, children!" he said in a very lively voice. The kids looked up from their books. "Today I am going to tell you the story of Anansi, the spider man."

"Spiderman!" A small boy cried out excitedly.

"But this isn't the comic book webslinger you know," Ogden told him. "This is a tale from Africa, where my relatives came from long ago."

"Is that why your skin is so dark?" a tiny blonde girl called out.

Ogden clapped his hands as if she'd said a brilliant thing. "Exactly right!"

Within minutes Ogden was acting out an African folktale. He had the kids on their feet, each of them playing the part of a different jungle animal. Katie snapped so many pictures, she used up all of her film.

In the end, the kids laughed and clapped with all their strength. Bowing, his face beaming, Ogden backed out the door. Katie ran after him. "You were wonderful!" she declared sincerely.

"Every week I see those poor kids looking so bored in

there. I've been wanting to do something for them for a while. I hope they liked it."

"They loved it!" Katie cried. "And I got great pictures."

As they stood in front of the library, a black limousine rolled silently along the street. The back window rolled down, and Molly stuck her head out. "Hey, Katie," she cried, waving.

"I'd better go." Ogden excused himself.

"You don't have to," Katie protested, but Ogden walked off with a brisk wave of his hand.

"Bye!" Katie called after him before joining Molly at the curb.

"Who was that?" Molly asked.

"A man I met at Come On Inn the other day."

Molly frowned with concern. "Should you be talking to him? Is it safe?"

"Sure," Katie said confidently.

"How do you know?" Molly questioned.

"I don't, I guess," Katie admitted. "He seems really nice, though. I feel he's a nice person. Everyone at the soup kitchen likes him."

Molly pushed the door open. "Get in before you freeze." Katie climbed in, and Molly introduced her to the chauffeur, Seamus.

"Pleased to meet you," he said with a pleasant smile.

"You, too," she replied.

Molly told Katie that she was there shopping for party supplies. "I have to ask you something. What do you think of this? Mom wants to invite some of her Daughters of Heritage friends to this party, to make it a huge event."

"Would they all bring food for the food pantry?" Katie asked.

"Yes. They would donate money, too. They've adopted Come On Inn as their new charity. That's why she wants to be involved."

"Great!" Katie cried happily. "Let her do it. It would mean more food and money for the soup kitchen."

Molly shook her head skeptically. "Wouldn't the kids think it was dorky?"

"Some might. But most of them wouldn't care. There will be so many kids there that they're bound to have fun. It'll be like a winter carnival or something."

Molly nodded excitedly. "It *will* be like that. And if Mom gets involved, the party will be even better. She's a whiz at parties. She'll make sure there's better food and more to do. She's great at that."

"Definitely let her do it," Katie insisted.

"Okay." Molly seemed to hesitate before speaking. "Katie, do you think there's a chance this party will get me voted Most Popular?"

Katie thought a moment. "It might," she agreed. "At school kids are very psyched about this. But how come you care so much?"

"I want Matt back," Molly said firmly. "And I'm going to get him back at this party. You wait and see."

23

Christina sat cross-legged on the edge of her bed, staring blankly out the window. She couldn't believe what Ashley had done. At first she was shocked and saddened when she realized that the angel's flashing eyes were not real. But the feeling inside her now was something more than disappointment. It was something deeper, worse.

She felt empty, as if something precious within her heart was now gone. What was it? Trust? Faith? She wasn't sure. But she could feel the hole inside her heart where it had once been, and she ached to have it back again.

Someone knocked at her door. "It's me, Ashley," said the voice on the other side.

"Go away."

"Christina, let me in," Ashley demanded. "I want to talk to you."

"It's open," Christina grumbled, knowing Ashley wouldn't give up. Although Ashley was the last person she wanted to see right now, it seemed she had no choice.

Ashley pushed the door open and took several steps into the room. She stared at Christina with a hard, blank expression. Christina did not return her gaze. "Do you have my remote?"

Turning slowly toward her, Christina jerked her head toward the top of her dresser, where the small black remote sat.

Ashley walked across the room, picked the remote up, and shoved it into her jacket pocket. "I figured you must have it. I dropped it when I fell, and you picked it up, didn't you?"

Christina nodded and Ashley nodded back. "Well, what are you waiting for?" Christina sneered after an unbearable moment of silence between them. "Don't you have a miracle to perform?"

"Stop it, Christina," Ashley said harshly. "You don't know why I—"

"Yes, I do." Christina cut her off angrily. "You did it for the ranch, so you think that makes everything all right. All the people you deceived—including me—don't matter because you did it for the ranch. You don't have to explain. I know how you think. Tell me, Ashley . . . did you build the angel yourself, too? Did you get up in the middle of the night and somehow whip her together, as well?"

Ashley stepped forward. "No. Of course not! The angel was there. But that night when I discovered her, I believed she was sent to help the ranch. You know how bad things are."

"How convenient for you!" Christina hooted, her voice filled with contempt.

"It's true!" Ashley insisted. "That's what I'd asked for out there on the Angel's Crossing Bridge. And a few hours later the snow angel appeared. What else could I believe?"

Christina laughed bitterly, turning away from Ashley and staring back out the window. "All right, say that was even true. Say the angel appeared just to help the ranch become famous. What happened next? What could you have possibly been thinking? Did you have to help the angel along? Give her a boost? It wasn't enough that she was there?"

Ashley said nothing.

"I guess you know better than the angels," Christina added sarcastically.

"Maybe I shouldn't have used the remote to make the angel's eyes flash," Ashley admitted, shifting from foot to foot.

"Yeah, maybe not," Christina agreed. "That's an understatement."

"But, Christina, try to understand," Ashley pleaded. "I was there all by myself that night. I knew the angel was sent to help the ranch. Then I remembered seeing Jeremy's remote control car in the front hall closet that morning. I thought people would come to see her if she did something special."

"Oh, so you got the remote, gouged a hole in the angel's head, and stuck a toy car in there!" Christina spun toward her, no longer able to contain her fury. She couldn't believe any of this. It was too outrageous!

"Ashley, you dug a hole in her head. This miraculous angel appeared, and you dug a hole in her! How could you?"

"I patched the hole up." Ashley defended herself weakly.

"That's not the point!" Christina shouted. "Why didn't you leave her alone?"

"You know how the angels work," Ashley said passionately. "They give you the chance to help yourself. They don't do everything for you. Remember what Ned said on the bridge? We have choices. We all make choices."

Christina glared at her friend. "And you chose to be a fraud."

"No, I chose to bring attention to the ranch. To help my family. I didn't know the angel would attract so much attention on her own. I still can't believe so many people came to see her on Sunday morning. I thought I might need a miracle, something to help her along."

Christina shook her head sadly. She couldn't accept this explanation. "A fraud is a fraud, Ashley," she murmured. "A lie is a lie. I thought I knew you, but I see now that I don't."

"Oh, don't act so perfect with me," Ashley cried, stepping closer to the bed. "You're the one who went shooting your mouth off to Liz Parker after your mother told you not to. Why did you tell her about the angels? We all made a promise never to tell. What were you after? Fame?"

"Not fame! The truth! I thought I was telling the truth!"

Christina yelled, jumping to her feet, outraged. "How can you possibly compare what I did to deceiving the entire town?"

"Sometimes you really bug me, Christina! You think every word out of your mouth is the truth!" Ashley countered. "You think everything you say is the truth, all the time. No matter how crazy or illogical it is, if you say it, then it must be the truth. You're just the perfect little truth teller. But everyone doesn't think the same way you do. There isn't only your truth!"

"My truth is the only truth I know!" Christina shouted, her eyes filling with tears.

"Well, let me tell you something, Christina. A lot of the things you think—a lot of things you say—are just . . . just . . ." Ashley's face shone crimson with fury. "They're just stupid!"

For a moment, the two girls stood staring at each other, breathing hard, red-faced. "All I know, Ashley, is that you lied to me," Christina said finally, her voice deadly calm. "You fooled everyone. And that can't be right."

Ashley opened her mouth to speak, but she was so filled with rage that no words came out. She turned and stormed angrily out of the room.

Christina fell back hard against her bed, emotionally drained.

Ashley's harsh words played around and around in her head. Were all the beliefs Christina held—her beliefs in mysticism, the tarot, horoscopes, crystals, power spots—really wrong? Was all of it stupid? Had she been wrong all along?

Was she fooling herself about all of it, just the way she'd been wrong about the flashing eyes of the snow angel?

So very, very wrong about that.

24

On the following Saturday, Molly woke early. It was the day of the snow angel party. This last week of preparation had gone fast. But the party would be great. Everyone would have an amazing time.

After this she would surely be voted Most Popular. Matt would see her in the center of the limelight, and he'd want her back for certain. Hopefully, she'd even get the chance to speak to him today.

At breakfast, Molly slid into the booth with her buttered bagel and hot chocolate. Her mother buzzed around the kitchen, too excited and busy with last-minute details to eat.

All week long, she, Molly, and Joy had worked feverishly on the party. Now, this morning, Mrs. Morgan was already on the phone with the caterers. From her mother's side of the conversation, Molly could tell they were discussing the waiters who would serve at the party.

Inside there would be refreshments, and they'd have a waiting staff to serve.

Outside, waitresses and waiters would move around offering cups of hot chocolate to everyone participating in the many events. There'd be a snow sculpture contest, a snow shoe contest, a toboggan run, and a snowball-throwing booth.

Her mother's awesome inspiration was that the waiting staff would all be dressed as angels with white robes and wings worn over their coats. Molly thought it was a fabulous idea, and the caterer had agreed to it.

Mr. Morgan came into the kitchen holding a suitcase. It was Liam's. "What are you doing with that?" Molly asked.

"Bringing it upstairs to pack Liam's things," he replied.

"Why?" Molly asked.

"Liam's going home this evening," he said, heading out of the room.

"What do you mean?" Molly cried.

Mr. Morgan put the empty case down and turned to Molly. "Conor phoned this morning. He and Liam's mother miss the boy terribly. Conor asked me to put Liam on the next flight to Ireland."

"But you can't," Molly protested. "Not tonight."

"I don't have a choice." Mr. Morgan sighed. "I want Liam to stay too, Molly, but we have to honor his father's wishes." Mr. Morgan picked up the suitcase and started up the stairs.

Molly sat there. Her mind was racing. Liam couldn't go. If he left now, they'd have failed. He'd be going home just as messed up as when he arrived.

Leaving her breakfast on the table, Molly ran upstairs to the guest bedroom, where Liam sat on the bed, staring blankly while Mr. Morgan took clothing from the closet. "Can't he stay another week?" she asked her father.

"I'm afraid not. Although you and I want to keep Liam here, there's no reason he should stay longer. He hasn't improved."

"But what about his reaction to the angels?" Molly pressed. "We need more time to find out what that's about."

Mr. Morgan shook his head. "There are angels in Ireland, too."

"Please," Molly pleaded.

"Molly, if it were up to me, you know Liam could stay. But this is out of my hands. We've got two tickets all set, one for Liam and one for Seamus, who'll fly home with him."

Quietly, Molly sat on the bed next to Liam. She'd never get to know him now. Never be able to help him. She felt that somehow she was close to uncovering the key to reaching him—but time had run out. "I'm sorry you're leaving," she said to the boy. As she expected, he didn't acknowledge her words.

Yet she thought she noticed something different about him. It was his eyes. There was more light in them, just a bit more movement. It encouraged her to speak again. "You might like to come down to the party later if you're feeling up to it. But I suppose I should warn you, there will be waiters and waitresses dressed as angels. They might freak you out. I know how you feel about angels."

Joy appeared at the door. "Phone for you, Mr. Morgan. It's the Fitzroy Gallery in New York."

"Ah, good," Mr. Morgan said, laying some clothing at

the edge of the bed and leaving the room.

Molly sat gazing at Liam. She felt so frustrated at seeing him like this. Something inside told her that he wasn't really as buried within himself as he had been. He'd put up such a struggle when he'd seen the snow angel.

"What is it, Liam?" she asked impatiently. "Why do the angels make you so nuts? What happened? You can't just go on like this."

He sat, impassively staring past her.

Molly took hold of his arm. "Liam, I was in the hospital for a while," she confided quietly. "I was starving myself because I thought that somehow it was what I deserved. I thought I'd failed in some way, that my parents disapproved of me. And, for a while, I believed I could never get better."

She paused, visualizing herself in her hospital gown, looking so bony, gazing hopelessly out the hospital window. Just the way Liam gazed so despairingly now.

"But, Liam," she continued, "I got better. It happened because I started to fight for my life. I wanted a better life, and I've got it now. You have to fight, too, Liam. You have to fight your way past whatever is terrifying you."

He blinked, and his eyes shifted toward her.

"What has the angel got to do with your fear?" she asked in a passionate whisper. "Angels are good. An angel wouldn't hurt you. An angel inspired me to get better. Angels help, Liam. They don't hurt you. Angels help!"

Molly discovered that a mist of tears had come to her eyes as she spoke. Why couldn't she get through to him?

Oh, of course she couldn't. Brilliant doctors and

psychiatrists had tried to reach him and failed. What made her think she could?

It was just that she'd stumbled onto this angel connection, and it seemed to have brought her closer than anyone else had gotten so far.

But, apparently, it wasn't close enough.

With a deep sigh, Molly slid off the bed. "I'm sorry you're leaving, anyway," she mumbled. "It would have been nice to get to know you—the real you."

She headed toward the door to leave. An awful croaking sound made her whirl around.

Had Liam made that sound?

She stepped back toward him with cautious steps, almost as if she feared that too much noise would send him scurrying inside himself once again.

She reached the side of the bed. "Did you say something?" she asked carefully.

"She tried to help," Liam said in that same rasping tone. "She tried but I was afraid."

Her heart pounding, Molly sat at the edge of the bed. "Who tried to help? An angel?"

Liam nodded. "I was afraid."

"Afraid of what? The angel?"

"The horse," Liam whispered. "Brian's horse was so wild. The storm scared her." He began trembling. Molly remembered how whenever Liam saw a picture of an angel, he had said he couldn't do something.

"What couldn't you do?" she asked softly.

"I couldn't do what the angel wanted me to do. She held the reins of Brian's horse. She told me to come take them."

"But you were too scared?" Molly supplied.

He nodded. "Even when the horse reared up over the cliff, she held the reins. She gestured to me with her hands. But I was afraid the horse would drag me over the cliff."

"And you didn't believe she'd take care of you," Molly said as a tear rolled down her cheek.

"Then the angel disappeared and the horse crashed down with Brian. That scared my horse, and he spooked, too. He threw me against the rocks. When I woke up, I was alone."

Liam began crying, deep, cleansing sobs that racked his body.

Molly put her arms around him, holding him as tightly as she could.

25

"**W**ow, look at this party," Ashley commented as she and Katie walked up to Molly's house several hours later.

The vast, sloping yard was already filled with people, kids and adults. Rock music blasted through huge speakers set up on long metal poles. Fluffy cotton clouds dotted with hundreds of golden stars were strung through the bare trees. The waiting staff in their angel outfits moved noiselessly through the crowd as they carried golden trays piled high with food. The scene looked magical.

"It's awesome," Katie agreed. "How come Christina didn't come over with us? Are you two still not speaking?"

"Still not speaking," Ashley admitted. "But I'd rather not talk about it. Let's find Molly and enjoy the party."

"If you say so," Katie agreed. "But this is driving me crazy. Why won't either of you tell me what the fight is about?"

"It's personal. Kind of hard to explain," was all Ashley could manage.

"That's exactly what Christina said when I asked her," Katie cried, throwing her arms wide with frustration. "I wish I knew what was going on. Molly's mad at Christina. Christina is mad at you. And even though I'm not mad at anyone, you guys won't talk to me! I've never seen Christina so bummed out."

"I know, but there's nothing I can do," Ashley said quietly. This had probably been the worst week of her life. She was overwhelmed with guilt over what she'd done, and every day she had to see Christina, who wore this dead, disillusioned expression on her face. Whenever Ashley had tried to talk to her this week, Christina had looked at her, said nothing, and walked away. Ashley felt as if she had not only fooled people over the angel, but that she'd somehow destroyed Christina's faith in the world. That seemed the worst part of all.

Ashley didn't know how to make up for what had happened. She'd run home the night of their fight and thrown the remote in the hall closet. There hadn't been another flashing eyes "miracle" since then, although people still kept coming to see the angel and waiting for her eyes to flash.

Ironically, people jumped to the conclusion that the angel's eyes had stopped flashing because people weren't being kind enough to one another. This idea set off a flood of good works around Pine Ridge and even into Miller's Creek. People donated money, clothing, food, and time to their needy neighbors as never before. Overnight, the sleepy little town of Pine Ridge had become the most charitable, friendly—and happy— place imaginable.

"Is Christina even coming to the party?" Katie asked, breaking into Ashley's thoughts.

"I don't know," Ashley said honestly. "We're not talking. Remember?"

"How could I forget?" Katie grumbled, rolling her eyes.

"I know all this fighting must be a pain for you, but I don't know what else to do," Ashley apologized. "Christina won't speak to me, so I can't fix it. Let's just forget about it for now."

They walked down the cobblestone driveway along the side of the house. Parked close to the throng of guests in the backyard was the WPNE news van. "I can't believe this party is so major that the media are covering it," Katie commented.

"Mrs. Morgan is a pretty big socialite around here," Ashley said. "All her parties are big news, especially her charity events." Ashley raised the string bag in which she carried her two cans of corn. "And this is a charity event."

Katie squeezed her paper bag holding the cans of corned beef hash she'd brought and nodded. "That's true. The publicity should really help Come On Inn, too."

Surveying the party, Ashley noticed the WPNE announcer, Tammy Jacobs, waving for her to come over. The woman stood next to Mrs. Morgan in front of a gigantic stack of donated canned food. Molly's mother was beaming. She was obviously happy that her party was a newsworthy event. Ashley and Katie made their way over.

"Girls, I'm so glad to see you." Tammy greeted them, beckoning for them to come closer so they'd be before the camera. Facing the cameraman, Tammy introduced Katie as the girl who, she'd been told, had inspired this food drive. She introduced Ashley as living on the Pine Manor Ranch, home of the miraculous snow angel.

Katie got the chance to speak about the good work being done at Come On Inn. While she talked, Ashley gazed around the party, looking to see who was there.

She spotted Molly deep in conversation with Matt. They were standing beside a long table loaded with steaming chafing dishes, and they both looked very serious. She wondered what they could be saying.

All around, serving "angels" offered warming cups of creamy hot chocolate to the party guests. More and more people were arriving. Ashley noticed that many carried lots of cans of food. *People are so generous when they feel inspired,* she thought. Now, clearly, they were inspired.

The presence of the angel had inspired them, of course. But what had really motivated people was the mysterious person who'd been doing good works around town. He or she had been the one to start this chain of kindness with the book donation at Children's House, and the people of Pine Ridge had continued doing good things. Who could it be? Was it an angel? Were Ned, Norma, and Edwina behind this? Or was it the snow angel?

"And Ashley." Tammy's voice cut through Ashley's thoughts. "I hear the snow angel's eyes have stopped flashing . . ."

As the woman spoke, Ashley sensed someone staring

at her. She turned and spotted Christina standing by a bare fruit tree, looking at Ashley with piercing, searching eyes.

"Do you have any thoughts about why the angel is no longer performing this miraculous feat?" Tammy continued.

Ashley looked at Christina and then back at the announcer. Everyone was waiting for her answer. She stood there for a long moment, struggling with herself. Then a slight smile formed at the corners of her mouth. She knew what she had to do.

"Yes, I know," she admitted in a quivering voice. "The eyes stopped flashing because I stopped making them flash."

A horrified gasp rose up among the small group of people standing nearby.

"What are you saying?" Tammy asked, eyes narrowed. "Has this all been a horrible hoax?"

"No, just the eye-flashing part," Ashley said, her voice still shaking. "I did that with a remote control. The angel is real."

The next thing Ashley knew, Katie was stepping in front of her. "And it certainly was a brilliant idea." She spoke to Tammy in a bright, cheerful voice. "Ashley knew that Come On Inn could use community support, and what better way to get it than to bring Pine Ridge together for this great cause."

"I suppose," Tammy conceded weakly as she signaled her cameraman to stop filming.

26

"So, you see, Molly, Christina won't even have anything to do with me as long as she thinks you care," Matt said to Molly.

"I do care," Molly said petulantly. "What you're asking isn't fair."

"It is fair," Matt insisted. "In the last few months you only saw me when you weren't doing something with your friends. You've made some great new friends, Molly, and you should spend time with them. I hope we'll always be friends, and I'll always care about you. But face it, as a boyfriend, I just wasn't that important to you."

"Oh, this is too much," Molly fumed as she turned away. "I won't do it."

"Molly, you know you would have broken up with me if I hadn't done it first," Matt reasoned. "We weren't going anywhere, and we don't even like the same things. We're too different."

Molly didn't want to hear any more of this. She

stormed away from Matt. How could he ask her to tell Christina it was all right for her to go out with him? The nerve! The insensitivity! When Matt had said he needed to speak with her, Molly's expectations had soared. Here they were not even an hour into the party, and her plan had worked like a charm. Or so she'd thought. Then he'd hit her with this unbelievable request—and he'd expected her to go along with it! It was like having a bucket of icicles dumped on her head.

As she stormed across the lawn, she witnessed another unexpected scene. Christina and Ashley were hugging and laughing. She'd thought they weren't even speaking.

Molly's head felt as though it were spinning. She had to get away from all these people. She needed a few minutes to collect her thoughts. Going in the back door, she ran through the guests standing in the kitchen and grabbed her skates from the front hall.

Heading out the front door, she encountered Seamus, the chauffeur, loading luggage into the limo. "Escaping from the party?" he inquired.

"I just need some time alone to think," she replied quickly without stopping. "And I think best when I'm skating."

"Careful on that ice," Seamus called after her.

"Sure," Molly answered absently without turning back to him.

She ducked around the outer rim of the party guests until she arrived at the pond. Molly breathed in the cold, crisp air and savored the relative quiet. She smiled. No one would think to look for her down here. Instantly, she felt a little better.

She put her foot on the stone bench, laced up her skates, then sailed out onto the pond.

She had so much to think about. Matt's request filled her head. Was there any truth in what he'd said? Was he really not important to her? She'd been telling herself he was, but was it the truth? Maybe she *had* taken him for granted the last six months or so. They really hadn't spent all that much time together lately.

Could it be true that she only wanted to keep him because she didn't like being dumped? Would she have broken off with him eventually if he hadn't done it first? Would she have?

Molly skated backward, then kicked her leg out and went into a spin. Her skate blades sprayed ice into the air as she turned.

When she came out of the turn, she still didn't know the answers to her many questions. How could she say what she would or wouldn't have done? How should she know?

She skated some more, drawing lazy figure eights on the ice with the blade of her skate. Her mind wandered to Liam. She recalled him shaking in her arms as he told her about the angel. Her father had come in shortly after that. He'd insisted on calling the doctor Liam had been seeing in the city.

While Mr. Morgan went to call, Liam had settled back on his pillow and drifted off to sleep. That's where Molly had left him.

The poor guy, Molly thought. He'd been through so much guilt and pain. But who could blame him for not following the angel's orders? It wasn't every day a person met an angel. He might not have even trusted his own eyes.

What could help him now? Certainly he'd made a huge breakthrough by talking about what happened up on the cliffs that day. Was it enough, though? Would it be enough to bring him back to a full, real life? Or would he be a prisoner of his own guilt forever?

Molly was suddenly seized with the strong desire to go upstairs and check on Liam. She'd been so absorbed in the last-minute party preparations and Matt that she hadn't thought about him in several hours. But surely he was more important than any of this. She had to see how he was.

She skated hurriedly toward the far end of the pond. She was in the middle of the pond, when, without any warning, her foot crumpled beneath her. She cried out in pain, then realized she hadn't merely turned her ankle.

Molly's foot was quickly sinking into a patch of gray mush, a soft spot in the ice. Off balance, her arms flailing, she fell backward and crashed through the ice behind her.

The numbing cold of the water knocked the breath from her lungs. Frantically she tried to hold on to something, but the ice kept breaking away all along the rim of the hole she was in.

She opened her mouth to scream for help, but her voice was stifled by the rush of freezing water that poured in as her head plunged beneath the surface of the pond.

The weight of her skates pulled her down, farther and farther. Fired by sheer willpower, Molly bent and tore at the laces. She had to get these skates off; her life depended on it.

Bubbles of precious air escaped her lips, floating upward as she worked. How long could she last in this icy water? Not much longer, she guessed. The water was so frigid, it felt as if it were burning her skin, and her lungs ached for air.

One by one her skates floated free, then sunk deep into the pond. With her load lightened, Molly felt herself rise. She tried desperately to swim up to the water's surface, but it was almost impossible. The weight of her clothing and the cold made it too hard to move her arms and legs.

Then, like a miracle, a hand plunged into the water and seized her wrist. She was being lifted, lifted from the freezing water.

The cold burned her cheeks as she rose above the pond. Gasping for air, she looked up and saw Liam gazing down at her as he held firmly on to her wrist.

They rose higher and higher.

How could this be? Molly wondered. What was pulling them up?

Lifting her head past Liam's shoulder, she saw a shining angel, a man, with enormous golden wings. He was lying on the overhanging branch of the tree by the pond and reaching forward.

His face radiated an inner glow of love and caring. His

long, reddish hair flowed over his shoulders, and a soft yellow light shone from behind his head.

He was holding on to Liam's hand.

27

Katie wondered where everyone was rushing off to. Something was going on at the far end of the yard.

It was probably another contest, like the snowshoe contest that had just ended. There was going to be a toboggan run soon, she'd heard. Katie had been so busy since she got here that now she wanted to rest for a few minutes.

Perched on the end of a table, she absently watched the serving "angels" come and go. Katie had to give Mrs. Morgan credit. No one else in Pine Ridge could throw a party like this.

Katie spotted a familiar figure dressed in an angel robe walking across the snow-covered lawn.

Ogden. Had he gotten a job serving here?

She slid from the table and hurried toward him. Then she stopped short. He was near the pile of donated food, and his arms were loaded with cans.

Katie blinked hard, not wanting to believe what she was seeing. Was Ogden stealing food?

Sensing her gaze, Ogden turned and saw her. He quickly put down the cans, placing them next to the overflowing pile. With a jerky, anxious wave of his hand, he walked quickly away.

How could he steal the food people had donated to Come On Inn? That didn't fit with Katie's idea of who he was. Not a bit!

Her mind raced. Okay, maybe he needed it. But Come On Inn was there for him. He didn't have to steal. Not Ogden! Not the man she'd thought was so terrific.

Tears of disappointment burned in her eyes. All her doubts about people came flooding back to her. If Ogden was capable of doing something so horrible, why should Katie believe in anyone?

She felt so betrayed! But he wasn't getting away that easily. She wouldn't let him. At the very least, she'd tell him what she thought of him.

Katie broke into a run, following the route Ogden had taken. She spied his white angel robe as he ducked through some tall bushes.

She crashed into the bushes behind him. They scratched her cheeks as she tore her way through, but Katie was determined to talk to Ogden face-to-face.

When she got to the other side, she saw him walking quickly toward a large white Rolls Royce parked on the street. Whose car was that? Was he planning to steal it, too?

"Ogden!" she shouted.

The man froze, then slowly turned back to her.

She ran forward and caught up with him. His face

looked sorrowful as she approached. "Caught me," he said with a quick smile.

He's not going to charm his way out of this, Katie told herself, panting and not returning his smile.

"You wouldn't give away my little secret now, would you?" Ogden asked.

Katie's hands flew indignantly to her hips. "And I thought you were a student of life!" she blurted, all her disappointment in him spilling forth.

"I am!" Ogden replied, confusion clouding his face.

"Students of life don't steal from other people!" she shouted.

Ogden looked deeply into her eyes. At first, his expression was quizzical, then his face brightened, seeming to laugh at her.

"It's not funny," she insisted angrily.

Ogden walked to the car, pulled the back door open, and leaned inside. Katie was surprised that someone with such a fancy car would leave it unlocked. Perhaps Ogden had already picked the lock and was planning to steal the car, too.

"Ogden, don't," she objected. "You can't—" Before she could finish, Ogden turned around, holding a large can. He held it out to her. "What's this?" she asked, taking the can from him.

"Look for yourself," he demanded.

"Jones's Oven Baked Honey Yams." She read the red label on the yellow can. Below the words was a picture of a plate of orange yams.

"Turn it around," he prompted.

"Oh, wow!" Katie gasped. On the other side of the label

was a photo of Ogden's smiling face. Below his face were the words "You have the Ogden Angel Jones Guarantee!"

Slowly, the embarrassing truth dawned on Katie. "You weren't stealing these cans, were you? You were donating them."

"How could you think that I'd steal?" Ogden scolded.

"Because you're poor and don't have any food," Katie admitted, then screwed her face into a bewildered knot. "But . . . are you really poor?"

"Check the license plate of that car," Ogden said, nodding toward the Rolls Royce.

The plate said: O-Angel-J. "That's yours?" Katie cried, aghast.

Ogden nodded.

"Why did you lie to me?" Katie asked.

"I didn't lie," Ogden insisted. "I make a lot of money selling yams the way my grandma used to make them. She'd smother them in honey and bake them until they were golden. I used to love sitting in her kitchen, watching her make yams. When I got older, she gave me her secret recipe. Even though my yams taste great, I never did get that recipe exactly right. Grandma must have added a bit more love than I do," Ogden said with a smile.

"I didn't lie when I said I was a cook, and I didn't lie when I said I fired myself. Running that company was making me rich, but it wasn't making me happy. So I put my nephew in charge and I set out to be a student of life, like I'd always wanted to be."

"Why are you wearing that angel costume?" Katie asked.

Ogden laughed. "So no one would notice me. I wanted to slip in, add my yams to the pile, and slip out."

With a flash of insight, Katie suddenly understood what had been happening. "Are you the person who's been doing all the good things around town, donating books and food and all?"

Ogden shrugged. "That's my pleasure. I drive into a town, get to know what needs doing, and do a little of it. The townspeople always do the rest. People are good, Katie, but sometimes they need a little push."

"You mean, you set off a chain reaction, just like what's happened in Pine Ridge."

"It almost always works," Ogden admitted with a grin. "I read about your snow angel in the paper, and it brought me here to Pine Ridge. That's some beautiful angel. What a gift."

"You're not a . . . a . . . you know?" Katie stammered, suddenly wondering if Ogden himself were an angel.

"A what?" Ogden asked.

"An angel," Katie blurted.

He hooted with laughter. "Just my middle name. Nope, I'm just a lucky old man who wants to spread the luck around." He pulled the angel robe up over his head and handed it to Katie. Underneath he wore white jeans and a heavy white sweatshirt.

"I think you're an angel," Katie said, smiling at him.

"It's been great knowing you, Katie, my girl," he said, returning her smile. "And I still say you're a deep thinker. Just remember to take a break once in a while and have some fun, too."

"I will," Katie agreed.

Ogden pulled a chain of keys from his pants pocket. "Time for me to be rolling along."

Katie stood, holding the yellow can of yams until Ogden's car was out of sight. Then, smiling, she turned to look back at the party going on on the other side of the hedges.

It seemed oddly quiet back there. She started walking back, curious to see where everyone had gone.

28

Molly lay on the living room couch, bundled in blankets. Only now was she starting to sort out what had happened. From the moment Liam pulled her from the ice, everything had happened so fast.

First, they were hanging there in the air. Then, suddenly, Seamus was there and he was carrying her back to the house in his powerful arms. Liam stayed beside him, holding her hand. People ran toward her from all over.

Then her parents appeared, her mother frantic, her father calm but concerned.

Blankets were thrown over her. The family doctor arrived and checked her. She'd be all right, he said, but they should keep her warm, get some warm fluids into her, and bring her to his office Monday morning for a complete checkup.

Liam came into the room and sat on the edge of the couch. He reached for her hand. "How are you feeling?" he asked.

"Still cold," she said, forcing a smile. "How did you find me?"

"I decided to try out your party, but I didn't know where you were. Seamus told me you'd gone skating. It was he who directed me down to the pond. As I was walking across the lawn, I saw you crash through the ice."

"Liam," Molly said, leaning forward. She winced. A throbbing ache came into her head as she moved, but she tried to ignore it. "Liam, did you see the angel?"

The boy nodded solemnly. "He was standing over the hole where you went under. He waved to me to come out and get you. I was scared the ice would break under me, too."

"But you went, anyway," Molly said, her voice soft.

Again Liam nodded. "I decided that this time I'd better trust the angel."

"And he held us up," Molly supplied.

"Yes, he did." Liam crunched his eyes shut, as if fighting back tears. "He did," he said again in a thick voice.

Molly reached forward and placed her free hand over his. "Thank you, Liam." She spoke from her heart. "Everything is going to be all right now. Somehow I know it is."

* * *

Molly slept on the couch and awoke several hours later feeling much better. The deep cold had gone out of her, and her head had finally stopped pounding. There was now only a dull ache behind her eyes.

"Do you feel well enough to see anyone?" asked her

father, who'd been sitting beside her in an armchair as she slept.

When she nodded, Christina, Katie, and Ashley were the first people he let in. "I'll go and help your mother clean up. The party was a huge success, Molly," he said with a smile as he left the room.

Christina was the first to rush to her side. "I know you're not speaking to me," she said. "But you have to. Forget about Matt, okay? I'm not going to see him, not if it upsets you."

"It's okay," Molly said, taking Christina's hand. "You can go out with him. It's all right with me."

"No, I won't. I won't," Christina said, shaking her head. "It's not more important than your friendship. I realize that now."

"I talked to Matt about it," Molly said. "He was right. I only wanted him back because he broke up with me. He and I weren't really that close anymore. You and Matt are perfect for each other."

"Still," Christina insisted. "I don't know."

"Why don't you just wait and see what happens?" Ashley suggested.

"Good idea," Molly agreed. "But it would be all right with me." She looked at her friends, their wonderful, concerned faces. How could she have ever doubted the sincerity of their friendship? What a loss it would have been if she'd thrown that away. "I'm sorry, guys. I've been sort of a jerk lately," she apologized.

"We've all been sort of jerks," Ashley said.

"Speak for yourself," Katie barked with a wry smile. "I wasn't mad at anyone."

"Okay. I've been sort of a jerk," Ashley amended. She told Molly, who didn't yet know, how she planted the remote control light with the flashing headlights inside the angel.

"But you did such a brave thing by admitting it on TV," Christina said, her eyes shining with admiration.

"Yeah, but I probably ruined everyone's faith in the angel," Ashley said unhappily.

"You didn't ruin my faith," Christina told her. "All last week I thought I'd been wrong about everything. But I wasn't. The angel wasn't a fraud. The angel's appearance really is something special. She appeared. That's enough. Even if her eyes didn't really flash, I learned something very important."

"What?" Molly asked.

"Well, I learned that some things are frauds. I should be more careful about what I believe. I can't just jump into accepting everything that comes along, and I can't expect everyone to think the same way I do."

"That's true!" Katie concurred enthusiastically.

"But some things are real, too. The world is full of miraculous things, like the snow angel and our angels," Christina finished.

"And Ogden A. Jones," Katie murmured, before filling them in on what had happened with Ogden. "He was the mysterious benefactor all along."

"And he's just a person," Molly added. "People can be miraculous sometimes, too, I suppose."

"It's true," Katie admitted. "Maybe I've been too hard on people."

"I hope people don't lose hope because of what I did," Ashley fretted.

"I don't think they will," Katie said thoughtfully. "The angel is a miracle. She brought Ogden here. And the good Ogden did has spread."

At that moment, Mrs. Morgan came down the stairs with Liam behind her. "You're leaving?" Molly cried. "I wanted to go to the airport with you."

Mr. Morgan stepped back into the room. "No. You're too weak," he said. "Seamus and I will take Liam to the airport, and Seamus will travel back to Ireland with him. Franklin's flight arrives in two hours. I'll ride home with him."

Molly tried to lift herself from the couch, but fell back from weakness. Liam came over to her. "Thank you, Molly," he said, wrapping her in a bear hug. "I never would have made it without you. I know I've got a long way to go, but I'll be fine thanks to you."

"No—thank you," Molly objected, squeezing back. "You saved my life."

Releasing his grasp, Liam shook his head. "You saved mine first," he said, gazing into her eyes. "I won't forget you."

"And I won't forget you," she replied sincerely. "I'll write."

For the first time, Molly saw Liam's face light with a smile. How handsome he looked when he smiled—handsome and happy. "I'll write back," he assured her warmly.

Seamus came in the front door. "Ready to go, sir?" he asked cheerfully as he winked at Molly. "Feeling better, Molly?"

"Yes. Thank you," she replied. "Thank you for everything."

"My pleasure." Picking up Liam's suitcase, he ushered the boy out the door.

"Help me to the window," Molly asked her friends. Katie lifted her, and Ashley helped from the other side. Christina stood behind Molly in case she stumbled. Together, they moved to the window, pushing aside the drapes.

Liam stood beside the gleaming black limousine and waved. The girls waved back and watched him climb into the back.

Seamus put Liam's bag into the trunk, closed the lid, and went to the driver's-side door. He looked up at the girls and waved.

The girls were struck silent at the sight before them. A glorious, broad-shouldered angel with streaming red hair, dressed in green robes, stood by the limo, waving. Huge golden wings fanned around him, and brilliant light emanated from him.

Then he ducked into the limo, turned the key in the ignition, and was gone.

"Seamus," Molly whispered. "Mr. O'Legan's an angel. I didn't even realize." Molly silently hoped that Liam had seen him, too.

"Wait a minute," Katie cried. "What did you say his last name was?"

"O'Legan," Molly replied. "Why?"

"I get it!" Christina exclaimed. "'O'Legan' is an anagram. 'Legan' is 'angel.'"

In silent awe, the girls put their arms around one

another and continued to look out the window at the snow that had started to fall.

Katie was first to speak. "It seems that there are angels all around us—spirit angels, human angels—and they're with us all the time."

"Always," Ashley agreed quietly.

"And forever," Christina added. "Always and forever."

FOREVER ANGELS

by Suzanne Weyn

ASHLEY'S LOVE ANGEL

Will Ashley's first love break her heart?

Ashley always hoped she'd have a boy in her life. Now she's got two! Although strong, handsome Dar is much older, Ashley thinks he's the perfect guy. And she's sure Dar feels the same way about her.

But then Ashley meets Jason, a new boy in school. He's definitely not boyfriend material—he's quiet, shy, and he stutters. But Ashley can't stop thinking about him. And when she discovers his secret in the Pine Manor woods one day, she wonders if Jason may be more special than she thought.

0-8167-4202-2